"Are you always this sassy?"

"It's the outfit." Anna brushed against Ryan's body, making him wonder what her bountiful breasts would feel like naked against his chest. Her wicked tongue coaxed his mouth open.

Then the porch light went on.

"Darn." Her teeth nipped his lip in frustration before she twisted out of reach. She scowled at the shadow in the front window of her apartment. "Would you like to come inside?"

The body screamed yes, but the mind waved a caution flag. Ryan was convinced he could find peace and comfort in Anna's home. But at what price?

He wasn't positive he had strength left to guard his heart.

Dear Reader,

9/11. A series of coordinated suicide terrorist attacks upon the United States, predominantly targeting civilians, carried out on Tuesday, September 11, 2001.

Every American was affected by the horrific events of that day, whether directly or indirectly. In the aftermath of the attacks, stories of valor, courage and bravery beyond our imagination emerged from the rubble. Survival stories, they were called. After reading dozens of these accounts, I wondered, *Where are these people now? What have they done with their lives? Have their lives changed for better or worse?*

The hero of my story, Ryan McKade, is a survivor of 9/11. That day altered his life in ways he could never have imagined. Coaxed from his self-imposed isolation by his meddling grandfather, Ryan finds himself having to confront his greatest fear—living. Luckily, Ryan meets Anastazia Nowakowski, who helps heal his ravaged heart and teaches him that bravery lies in one's ability to accept oneself.

I hope you enjoy reading Ryan and Anna's story—the last of my THE MCKADE BROTHERS series. If you missed *Aaron Under Construction* or *Nelson in Command*, the books can be ordered from online retailers or through local bookstores.

Drop me a note and tell me what you think of the McKade men, as I love hearing from readers. I can be reached at www.marinthomas.com.

Happy reading!

Marin

RYAN'S RENOVATION
Marin Thomas

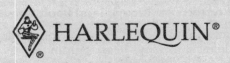

HARLEQUIN®

TORONTO • NEW YORK • LONDON
AMSTERDAM • PARIS • SYDNEY • HAMBURG
STOCKHOLM • ATHENS • TOKYO • MILAN • MADRID
PRAGUE • WARSAW • BUDAPEST • AUCKLAND

ISBN-13: 978-0-373-75179-2
ISBN-10:   0-373-75179-6

RYAN'S RENOVATION

ABOUT THE AUTHOR

Typical of small-town kids, all Marin Thomas, born in Janesville, Wisconsin, could think about was how to leave after she graduated from high school.

Her six-foot-one-inch height was her ticket out. She accepted a basketball scholarship at the University of Missouri in Columbia, where she studied journalism. After two years, she transferred to U of A at Tucson, where she played center for the Lady Wildcats. While at Arizona, she developed an interest in fiction writing and obtained a B.A. in radio-television. Marin was inducted in May 2005 into the Janesville Sports Hall of Fame for her basketball accomplishments.

Her husband's career in public relations has taken them to Arizona, California, New Jersey, Colorado, Texas and Illinois, where she currently calls Chicago her home. Marin can now boast that she's seen what's "out there." Amazingly enough, she's a living testament to the old adage "You can take the girl out of the small town, but you can't take the small town out of the girl." Her heart still lies in small-town life, which she loves to write about in her books.

Books by Marin Thomas

HARLEQUIN AMERICAN ROMANCE
1024—THE COWBOY AND THE BRIDE
1050—DADDY BY CHOICE
1079—HOMEWARD BOUND
1124—AARON UNDER CONSTRUCTION*
1148—NELSON IN COMMAND*

*The McKade Brothers

Mom

You sprouted your angel wings too early and took us by surprise. But I guess you had things to do and places to see. I close my eyes and imagine you happily managing your craft boutique, the Purple Plum. I see your gardens are in full bloom and my latest release is on your bedside table. And if I'm not mistaken, there's a cowboy at your door, who's come a-courtin'.

I feel you around me every day, touching me with your loving spirit. I miss you so much, Mom.

Chapter One

Ryan McKade, president of the New York City branch of McKade Import-Export, stood on the chipped-concrete sidewalk in north central Queens and studied the 1950s brick-and-stone building that housed Parnell Brothers Rubbish Removal. As a five-year-old he might have dreamed of becoming a garbageman, but he was thirty-six years old, for God's sake—what had his grandfather been thinking?

The building reminded him of an old fire station. An extra-wide automatic door, with windows along the top half, faced the street. Two sanitation trucks sat parked inside, Parnell Bros. Inc. 1952 painted in bold black lettering across the red brick above the doors. A smaller entrance to the right of the garage area had the word Office etched into the glass pane.

A dingy American flag sagged from a pole—a victim of air pollution. Ryan had noticed the difference in air quality the moment he'd stepped off the train. He was accustomed to cab exhaust across the East River in Manhattan. Here in the industrial Flushing area, a heavy metallic taste flavored the air. Faded plastic flowers filled a pot next to a dented garbage can chained to the downspout against the building. Ryan commiserated with the fake yellow daisies—looking as out of place as he felt.

The sky rumbled for the third time in as many minutes. Flushing was home to LaGuardia Airport. During the pre–9/11 years, Ryan had attended several Mets baseball games at Shea Stadium, which had been built in the flight path of the airport. It was a toss-up what annoyed the visiting team more—the rowdy fans or the deafening air traffic.

A quick check of his watch convinced him that if he ran the four blocks to the train station he could catch the M line and return to his Wall Street office in Lower Manhattan within the hour. Or hire a cab ride across the Queensboro Bridge and arrive there in forty-five minutes.

Grandfather's right. You are *a coward.*

Arguing with the ninety-one-year-old man had accomplished nothing. The family patriarch had embarked on a mission to teach each of his grandsons a life lesson before leaving the earth and he'd refused to allow Ryan to negotiate a way out of his. Not that Ryan had really tried. He owed his grandfather big-time.

Patrick McKade had raised him and his brothers, Nelson and Aaron, after their parents had perished in a private plane crash when Ryan was two. But more important, his grandfather had never left Ryan's hospital bedside while he'd recovered from injuries sustained the day terrorists attacked the World Trade Center. Not even Ryan's wife had had the fortitude to stick by him.

In truth, Ryan hadn't been upset with the old man's crazy scheme as much as he'd been devastated by the lesson he believed Ryan needed to learn—*bravery*. Evidently, rescuing a woman from the North Tower had failed to gain him hero status. Ryan believed it was no coincidence that his grandfather had arranged for him to begin the new job on September 11—six years post–9/11.

"Life goes on," his grandfather had argued.

Maybe for people who'd watched the disaster unfold on television inside their homes. But for the unlucky ones, those who'd lived through the hellish hours of the attack, the memories never faded. They were always present...in the corners of his mind. In the eyes that stared back at him in the mirror. In the scars that hid beneath his clothes.

The old man's right. You've got a yellow streak the length of the Holland Tunnel running along your spine.

A cool September morning breeze threatened to turn the beads of sweat on Ryan's brow into flecks of frost. As much as he found the idea of hauling garbage for three months distasteful, the prospect of socializing with people made his stomach spasm. He preferred to work alone. Isolated from his staff. Isolated from the world.

"Can I help you?"

Startled, Ryan shifted his gaze from the plastic daisies to the head poking out the office door.

"You've been standing on the sidewalk for ten minutes." The woman smiled.

Only a perpetually cheerful person would beam brightly at 7:00 a.m. on a Monday morning.

Run or stay. What's it going to be?

Damn. "I believe I've found the right place."

Her head edged farther out the door, displaying a prominent nose no one would dare characterize as feminine. Ryan shifted his attention to her eyes. Deep blue pools, sparkling with humor.

"You must be the new hire." Shoving the door open wide, she waved him in.

He entered the office, then shook the hand she offered, noting her no-nonsense grip. "Ryan Jones." He perused the length of her body—a far cry from the skinny model types he'd dated in college. This lady had meat on her bones. Curves his former wife would have spent hours in the gym ridding herself of.

"Anastazia Nowakowski. Pleasure to meet you."

Anastazia Nowakowski. Quite a mouthful.

"The guys call me Anna." Pointing to a refreshment table across the room, she offered, "Coffee?"

"No, thank you." Just when he thought her smile couldn't beam any wider…he winced, expecting her lips to crack.

The overhead fluorescent lights bounced off her pearly whites, and he noticed her two front teeth faced inward, reminding him of an open book. He never paid attention to smiles, but this lady's was warm and pretty. Too bad her effort was wasted on him.

A sparkly clip secured a mop of honey-blond hair to the top of her head. The style accentuated her high European cheekbones and strong jawline. Taken separately, the woman's features weren't beautiful. But put together…Anastazia Nowakowski's face was striking. Although shorter than Ryan's six-foot height by a good four inches, she was nothing if not intriguing. Too bad he'd sworn off women years ago when his wife served him divorce papers.

"Is Mr. Parnell in?" The sooner he escaped the clutches of Ms. Sunshine the better.

"I'm afraid not. Bobby's been busier than usual the past couple of months. I've had to take over most of his responsibilities." She shuffled through a stack of folders on her desk. "I have your file right here."

He had a file already?

"Usually, new employees interview with me prior to Bobby hiring them." *Pause.*

Had she hoped Ryan would explain how he'd managed to get the job without going through the proper channels? Seconds ticked by. He had no intention of explaining his grandfather's shenanigans, or how he'd been forced to become a garbageman in order to learn how to be brave.

After a lengthy silence, she added, "I must have been out to lunch when you were interviewed."

Interviewed? Yeah, right. If Ryan hadn't been ticked off at his grandfather over the whole bravery thing, he might have questioned the old man's a-friend-who-knew-someone-who-knew-someone-who-knew-the-owner explanation. Funny how the old man had a heck of a lot of friends with their tickers still beating.

Anna shoved the forms under the stapler, then smacked the top with her palm. "Bobby phoned a few minutes ago and informed me you were starting this morning." She motioned to the chair in front of the desk and...yep, smiled. *Again.*

Did she ever scowl? No normal human being was this happy *all* the time. Squelching the urge to say something to tick her off, he settled in the chair.

She scribbled his first name on the form, left a space, then wrote in his last name. "Middle initial?"

Although he'd been instructed not to use his real last name, Ryan hadn't been told not to use his real middle name. "T. Thomas."

"Social security number?"

He repeated the number, doubting she'd check its validity since he'd be employed such a short time with the company.

"Previous employment?"

Along with keeping his name confidential, he was not to mention his real occupation. His grandfather had insisted Ryan not receive special treatment because of who he was or where he worked. As if garbagemen read the business section of the *Times* each morning—besides, Ryan hadn't been in the news for over three years now. "Sales," he offered, hoping she'd skip specifics.

One light-brown eyebrow arched.

"Computer sales," he hedged.

The eyebrow drifted back into place, and she beamed as if she'd figured out the mystery of Ryan Jones. "Best Buy? Office Max?"

"Something like that," he muttered, wishing his grandfather was in the room so he could strangle the old man.

"Address?"

He offered one of his business P.O. box numbers and a Manhattan zip code.

If she recognized the postal code, she didn't let on. "Emergency contact?"

Ryan recited his grandfather's cell number—served the meddling old coot right if she called to verify Ryan's information.

"That's all I need." She slipped from behind the desk. "We have time for a quick tour before the others arrive."

Ryan beat her to the door and held it open. Her eyes rounded as if she wasn't accustomed to small courtesies.

They entered the garage area and Ryan recognized the two dump trucks he'd spotted from the street. One vehicle was loaded with a pile of construction debris, the other empty. Saws, drills, sledgehammers and various other tools hung from hooks along the back wall.

"Parnell Brothers is best known for their demolition

work. With more and more dual-income families moving into Queens, our teardown and cleanout services bring in a fair amount of money for the company."

"Teardowns?"

The question produced another smile from the boss lady. "You'd be surprised at the number of two-family brownstones being gutted and made into single-family residences."

"I assumed I'd be helping with garbage collection."

"We do that, too, for private businesses. The company also volunteers once a month to assist in a community cleanup program. It saddens me that people discard old furniture, broken bottles, tires and a million other trash items in empty lots."

If she was sad, why was she smiling? The secretary paused, as though expecting a comment. "I noticed a few bad areas when I got off the train," he mumbled.

"We're making progress though." *Smile.* "Are you up-to-date on your tetanus shot?"

After 9/11 he'd had enough needles shoved into him to cover every disease on the planet. "I'm good."

Opening a cupboard in the wall, she explained, "Most of the men prefer their own work gloves." She craned her neck to the side and checked his empty butt pocket. "Feel free to grab a pair to use."

"Dirty gloves go there." She motioned to a white basket under the workbench. "I launder them over the weekend." Anastazia Nowakowski was a woman of many talents—secretary, stand-in boss and mother hen.

Great. A smiling, smothering, mothering, hovering female—just what he didn't need.

"This is the locker room." She breezed through a door. A sickly sweet odor tickled his nostrils. The place didn't smell like any locker room he'd ever entered. He counted five air fresheners—Fruit Orchard, Apple Blossom, White Gardenia, Hibiscus and Fresh Meadow. How the heck did the men stand the stink?

Anna handed him a key and pointed to locker 23. "Joe Smith is next to you in 24. He's been with Parnell Brothers for three years. Until you, he was our newest employee."

Wondering if he could make her frown, Ryan scowled. *Nope.*

"Don't worry, Joe's a nice guy. You'll get along fine with him."

Huh? He'd better control his facial muscles, or he'd end up unintentionally offending everyone in the company.

"His father suffered a stroke not long ago, and Joe had to move back in with the family." She sighed, the rush of air from her mouth feathering across his forearm. "His younger brother got mixed up with a gang. Joe's been nagging Willie to get out. We're all worried about the teen."

Hoping to end Anna's commentary on Joe's family, Ryan remained silent. He had no intention of becoming buddy-buddy with any of his coworkers. The less familiar he was with the men, the easier to keep his distance. The trauma of 9/11 had wreaked havoc on his emotions. When the dust of destruction had cleared, a solid, frozen mass of emptiness had remained in his chest. He had nothing left to give to anyone.

"Eryk Gorski is in locker 18. He turned forty last week." Anna winked. "Whenever anyone has a birthday, I bake a cake and we celebrate."

Ryan's birthday was next week. *Yee-ha.*

"Next is Leon Bauer. He's forty-five and has been with Parnell Brothers the longest. Twenty years."

A twenty-year career in garbage? Ryan had to admire the man for sticking with the job that long.

"Leon hasn't missed more than a day or two of work in all those years." She leaned forward and whispered, "He can't stand staying at home. It's not his wife, Helga, but the other relatives who drive him crazy. Last time I asked, Leon confessed to thirteen people living in the three-bedroom home."

Her clean feminine scent messed with Ryan's concentration. In self-defense, he retreated a step, hoping the added space would clear his senses. "When do the other guys arrive?"

"Soon. Next to Leon is Patrick Felch," Anna said, continuing with the Parnell Brothers' family tree. "Ask Patrick to sing for you sometime."

Was she nuts?

"Patrick has a beautiful voice," Anna droned. "He's a member of St. Mary's choir. What church do you belong to, Ryan?"

He'd gone to Sunday services once after his post–9/11 release from the hospital. Mostly to rage at God for what had happened to him. He hadn't returned since. "Ah…"

Her face softened with understanding. "I say a prayer for all the men. I'll add you to my list."

Well, that was a first—a woman praying for him.

"He's miffed at Father Baynard because Father refused to forgive him at confession."

Who was miffed? And who was Father Baynard? Ryan was having a hell of a time following the conversation.

The throaty sound of her giggle squeezed his chest. "Patrick shouldn't have confessed that he'd had sex with a girl on their first date. The girl turned out to be Father Baynard's niece."

Ryan decided he'd better watch what *he* confessed around Miss Happy Chatty or the information was bound to leak out. By the end of his tour of duty at Parnell Brothers, the more than two million residents of Queens would learn everything about him, including the color of his BVDs.

"And finally, on the other side of Patrick is Antonio Moretti. He has two cute little boys. You should see him with his sons. He's such a good father."

An unexpected pain jolted Ryan. Would a time ever come that he'd hear the word *father* and *not* react?

"You should have plenty of room in the locker for an extra pair of clothes and shaving supplies. Depending on the job, the men sometimes shower before going home. If you run out of anything, I stock a few items in the storage closet." She opened a door across the room.

Travel-size bottles of shampoo, conditioner, shaving cream and soap were arranged in neat rows. *Pink* bath towels occupied the top shelf.

"First aid kit." She motioned to a red-and-white box. Then her finger moved to the bottom shelf. "If the bathroom needs more…it's right…" She slammed the door shut.

For the first time that morning Ryan wanted to grin. What an intriguing woman. Anna didn't mind repeating gossip about sex but discussing toilet paper turned her face Stop-sign red.

"The break room is through this door or the one in the hallway we passed earlier."

Secondhand furniture filled the lounge: a gray

Formica table, eight mismatched chairs, a television set, a plaid-print couch that sagged in the middle, an olive-green refrigerator, a countertop microwave and an automatic coffeemaker.

"The guys usually brown-bag it for lunch." She opened the cupboard above the sink. "Cream, sugar, salt and pepper packets." Next cupboard. "Paper plates, napkins, plastic spoons and forks." Refrigerator. "Condiments and help yourself to the jug of iced tea."

He nodded his thanks.

"Not much of a talker, are you?" Her smile didn't quite camouflage the note of disappointment in her voice.

If he'd quit caring what people thought of him years ago, why did her observation twist his gut into a knot? He shrugged.

She crossed the room to the chart on the wall.

"I post the next week's schedule by noon on Friday." She tapped a long pink fingernail against his name. "I marked you for a cleanout this week."

"Cleanout?"

"Compare it to spring-cleaning."

Spring-cleaning sounded like a woman's job.

His face must have shown his confusion because she smiled at him as if he were a dense child. "The home is off Fish Pond Road and we've been asked to gut it. The owner died and his children live in Florida."

"The family isn't handling the estate?"

"Mr. Kline was estranged from his family. His children want us to haul everything to the dump. I've already sorted through his belongings and donated what was useful to local charities."

"What's left to get rid of?"

"Several pieces of furniture. Then the carpet, the

cupboards, the light fixtures, toilets, sinks, tub, linoleum flooring, and in this case, the front porch has to be torn off the house and hauled away."

Spring-cleaning my... More of a demolition project. "So the house is going to be demolished?"

"Oh, no. A couple made an offer under the condition the place is ready for remodeling at closing." As if she'd finally run out of oxygen from talking nonstop for the past twenty-five minutes, Anna sucked in a noisy breath of air. "I believe I've covered everything."

And then some.

"Any questions, Ryan?"

"Who's the other Parnell brother?"

"Harold. He died of colon cancer two years ago."

"Sorry to hear that," Ryan mumbled.

"He handled the financial end of the business, and since his death Bobby's struggled with some cash-flow problems, but things will smooth out."

Meaning what—the business was in monetary trouble? What did he care? He'd be gone in three months.

"Any questions?" she asked.

"Payday?"

"Fridays." Her smile faltered—a first since they'd begun the tour. "May I ask you a question?"

A sliver of dread poked Ryan between the shoulder blades. "Sure."

Her blue eyes turned icy. "What's an uptown man such as yourself doing working for a trash company?"

WHEN RYAN JONES didn't immediately respond, Anna congratulated her instincts for being correct. The moment she'd clasped his hand and gazed into his eyes—probing brown eyes—she'd been certain he didn't hail from a neighborhood in Queens. As a matter of fact, she couldn't detect any of the five boroughs' accents in his speech, convincing her that there was much more to the new employee than met the eye.

"I'm taking a sabbatical from my other job," he offered.

"Sabbatical meaning…you've been sent here to fulfill a community-service sentence?" She crossed her arms over her chest. "DUI? Drug possession?" Not long ago she'd read a magazine article about white-collar employees often getting slapped with community service for breaking the law, while blue-collar workers ended up in jail for the same offense.

Ryan's mouth dropped open, affording Anna a glimpse of perfectly even white teeth—no fillings in his lower molars. She considered herself a good judge of character and decided his slack-jawed expression was genuine.

"I've never been arrested for anything in my life," he insisted.

Maybe she'd gone overboard with the drinking and drug accusations, but one could never be too careful. She took her job seriously and considered her coworkers family—she'd been looking out for their best interests. And truthfully, she didn't understand why Bobby had hired another employee when the company had trouble meeting payroll.

Nothing about Ryan Jones made sense. A person had a right to privacy, but honestly, the man needed to relax and loosen up. If not, his standoffishness might prevent him from being accepted by the other men. Maybe she should suggest a few pointers on friendliness—

Right then a buzzer sounded. "The crew's here." She slipped past Ryan, catching a whiff of cologne. Expensive. Not dime-store stuff. He smelled of sophisticated, refined male. In all her thirty-two years she'd never met a man who piqued her interest more than Ryan. "C'mon. I'll introduce you to everyone."

After she pressed a button on the garage wall, the heavy door rose, revealing five pairs of work boots, then five sets of jean-clad legs, five metal lunch boxes, five broad shoulders and, finally, five heads, four wearing baseball caps, the other bald as a bowling ball.

"Morning, guys," she greeted.

A chorus of "mornin'" bounced off the cement walls.

"Ryan Jones," she began, then indicated each man as she said his name. "Antonio Moretti."

"Tony," he corrected, stepping forward to shake Ryan's hand. "Only Anna gets away with calling me Antonio."

"Patrick Felch," she continued.

"Pat will do."

Ryan nodded. "Nice to meet you."

"Joe Smith and Eryk Gorski."

"Good morning." Ryan shook their hands.

Eryk shoved a copy of the daily newspaper under his arm and studied Ryan through narrowed eyes. "You look familiar."

When Ryan didn't comment, Anna continued. "And Leon Bauer."

Leon waved, then skimmed his palm over his bald head. A habit the dear man hadn't been able to break since the last few strands of hair had fallen out five years ago.

"I've given the new guy a tour of the station, assigned him a locker and explained the schedule. He's all yours now." The hint of uncertainty in Ryan's eyes tempted Anna to hang out in the garage a few more minutes, but work waited on her desk. "I'll check in with you later," she promised with an encouraging smile.

By the end of the week she'd find out everything about Ryan Jones—even if she had to use a chisel and a mallet to break through his stony facade.

Chapter Two

Tense as a cornered rabbit, Ryan shifted from one size-twelve foot to the other as five pairs of eyes studied him. He didn't appreciate the attention. And he didn't approve of his grandfather's motives—no matter how sincere.

"Jones, you'll be with Eryk and me," the bald man, Leon, announced, then headed to the break room, the others trailing behind.

Except Eryk. He continued to study Ryan. "I swear I've seen you before."

Maybe the other man had come across the newspaper photo of Ryan after 9/11. "I don't live around here."

After a thoughtful nod, Eryk walked off, leaving Ryan alone in the garage. He held his breath until the break-room door closed, then a powerful rush of air burst from his lungs, leaving him dizzy and shaky. He'd given presentations to a convention room full of peers and had never been this nervous.

Those were the times you enjoyed being the center of attention.

The lukewarm welcome from his coworkers convinced Ryan he needed a new game plan to endure the next three months. Something along the lines of…mind his own business, don't ask personal questions and where the company secretary–slash–boss lady was concerned…don't, under any circumstances begin a conversation. Aloofness was the key to survival.

"Have you ever worked construction?" Eryk asked, appearing out of nowhere.

"No." Ryan was wondering how to keep his guard up when a man wearing twenty-pound construction boots walked across a concrete floor without making a sound.

"Demolition?"

"Some." Ryan's one experience with destruction had been the night he'd torn apart his bedroom. By the time his anger, hurt and frustration had been exhausted, nothing salvageable remained—save for the memories of 9/11. Those were indestructible.

The break-room door banged against the brick wall. "Let's go." The furrows bracketing Leon's mouth deepened.

"Don't mind him," Eryk whispered. "He hasn't gotten a decent night's sleep in over a month since his daughter and son-in-law moved in with him."

Great. Apparently, Girl Friday wasn't the sole motor-mouth in the place. Leon slid onto the driver's seat of the empty dump truck. Ryan hustled to the storage cupboard and grabbed a pair of work gloves. Eryk stood by the passenger door, motioning for Ryan to hop in first.

"Anna said she was able to donate most of the furniture to nonprofit groups, so we might get away with one haul to the dump before we rip out the flooring and fixtures," Leon commented as the truck edged out of the bay and into the street.

"Good," Eryk grouched. "I'm dead tired after this weekend."

"Babysitting does that to you." Leon chuckled, jabbing Ryan's side with a bony elbow.

"I can't believe my sister-in-law talked my brother into having four kids. The brats ambush us when they come over."

Ryan refrained from adding to the exchange. He never engaged in guy-banter with his employees. Personal lives remained personal—in and out of the office.

"Your sister-in-law's a pretty woman. I doubt she was doing any talking in the bedroom." Another elbow landed against Ryan's side.

"Pretty or not, her kids are holy terrors," Eryk complained.

"So now they're her kids and not your brother's?"

"Hell, yes. She stays at home and raises them while my brother busts his ass to put food on the table." The truck stopped at a light. Eryk unrolled the window, hacked up a wad of phlegm and spit it at the pavement. "You got any kids, Jones?"

"No." Ryan fought off a pang of sadness at the memory of almost being a father. At least his siblings were making their grandfather happy in that department. His younger brother, Aaron, and his wife, Jennifer, were expecting their first child around Christmas. His elder brother, Nelson, had inherited a teenage son when he'd married his wife, Ellen.

"Count yourself lucky." Eryk interrupted Ryan's thoughts. "One weekend a month, Pam and I watch the nieces and nephews. We began six years ago when they were two, five, seven and ten." He snorted. "Hell, it was easy back then. Now the sixteen-year-old has a mouth meaner than a hooker's. Can't drag the thirteen-year-old away from his video games. The eleven-year-old's favorite expression is *make me*. And the eight-year-old—shoot, she's the best one in the bunch. Give her a box of Froot Loops and she's a happy camper."

The truck rolled into the intersection. "Then tell 'em you've had enough," Leon insisted.

"A couple of times Pam and I almost stopped babysitting," Eryk added.

"Why didn't you?" *Damn*. Ryan hadn't meant to voice the question.

"Guilt. My sister-in-law almost died during 9/11. That day changed my brother. Changed all of us."

Changed didn't begin to describe Ryan's transformation after the attack.

"Once a month, they go off alone somewhere," Eryk went on. "My brother's afraid each weekend might be the last he and his wife have together."

9/11 had forever changed thousands of peoples' lives. Many, like Ryan's, for worse, and some, like Eryk's sister-in-law's and brother's, for the better.

Leon slammed on the brakes when a car cut in front of them. "Anna says going off for a weekend is romantic."

"The woman insists peanut butter and jelly is romantic," Eryk grumbled.

"You're a good uncle. God will reward you in heaven."

Ryan used to believe in heaven, but after 9/11 he doubted he'd ever see the pearly gates.

"Good uncle, my ass. I put up with the hooligans because Pam wears her French-maid costume to bed Sunday night after the brats leave."

The bawdy comment startled Ryan but didn't stop Leon from adding, "My Helga wouldn't be caught dead in one of those sex getups. She locked me out of the bedroom for a month when I brought her a pink thong from Victoria's Secret for Valentine's Day. Accused me of being a pervert. Shoot, I'm old, but I ain't dead. I'm fond of her big ol' butt cheeks."

"What do your ladies wear, Jones?" Eryk asked.

Eyes trained on the dashboard, Ryan grunted, "I'm divorced." He had no desire to chat about women, sexy lingerie or butt cheeks.

Silence ensued. *About time.* After the next traffic light Leon turned on Fish Pond Road. Many of the homes were old and decrepit, but a few houses had been renovated, and one property had been demolished for new construction. Leon stopped the truck in the middle of the block, shifted into Reverse and backed into the driveway of a ramshackle two-story brick bungalow.

A rusted chain-link fence surrounded both the front and side yards. Apparently, the home had died along with the owner. Weeds had choked out the grass, and the bushes barely clung to life, refusing to shed their crusty brown leaves. Even the ceramic angel, with a broken wing and arms raised skyward, begged to be rescued from her desolate resting place.

As they piled out of the truck, Eryk cautioned, "Watch the porch steps. The second one's rotted."

Leon studied the damaged step. "We'll have to slide the heavier pieces off the end."

The inside of the house fared worse than the outside. Ryan gagged on the putrid air—a combination of mold, rodent droppings and cat feces.

"Jones, you take the second floor. Toss what you can onto the lawn. Eryk, clear out the garage. I'll be in the basement."

Pop. Creak. Snap. Ryan gingerly navigated the

stairs to the second floor. When he reached the landing, an object—big and black—dived at his head, and he ducked, losing his balance. The trip down the stairs lasted half as long as the climb up. Ryan bounced to a stop at the front door, shoulder throbbing and elbow on fire.

"What the hell happened?" Leon rushed into the room and gaped. "Stair give out?"

"Tripped." Damned if Ryan would admit a bat had scared the crap out of him. He accepted a hand up and swallowed a moan of pain.

"Maybe you'd better break out a window upstairs and drop the stuff into the yard," Leon suggested, then returned to the basement.

Two hours later, drenched in sweat and arms burning with exertion, Ryan wanted to quit. A half hour on the treadmill and a twenty-minute workout on the Bowflex machine three times a week hadn't prepared him for pulling up carpet, dismantling light fixtures and shoving mattresses through windows. Adding to his misery was the fact that he couldn't get Anna's face—her big nose, her blue eyes, her strong jaw—out of his ever-loving mind.

Wishing he'd thought to bring along a bottle of water, he rested his hands on his knees and sucked in large gulps of air. After a minute, the pinched feeling eased in his lungs and he returned to the first floor.

Time crawled as he joined Eryk in the garage and carried load after load to the front yard. Hefting an old car tire onto his shoulder, he wondered whether the old man would call a halt to this life lesson if Ryan collapsed from physical exhaustion. There was always a possibility…. He heaved a second tire onto his other shoulder and staggered along the driveway.

"BOSS SHOW UP?" Leon took a seat at the table in the break room. After the men called it quits, Leon stole a cup of coffee and a few minutes of tranquillity before heading home to a houseful of extended relatives.

Anna placed the creamer from the fridge next to Leon's elbow. "Bobby came in at noon, stayed an hour, then claimed he had a personal matter to attend to and left." She allowed Leon one minute of peace and quiet, then demanded, "Well?"

"Well, what?"

How did Helga put up with the man? Climbing all 102 floors of the Empire State Building would be less taxing than extracting information from Leon. "Ryan. Did he say where he lives?"

Ignoring the question, Leon winced. "I've got the knees of an eighty-year-old."

Guilt pricked Anna for badgering the poor man when he was obviously worn out. She fetched two ice packs from the freezer. While Leon adjusted the packs over his knees, Anna's thoughts drifted to Ryan.

The new employee had been on her mind all afternoon. Leon, Eryk and Ryan had returned to the station for lunch, but she'd been tied up on the phone with the company's CPA and hadn't had the opportunity to ask the anyone how things were going.

She blamed her preoccupation with Ryan, not because he was a new employee, but that he was handsome and exciting in a mysterious way. Of course, she didn't believe for a minute anything would develop between them, but a girl could dream, couldn't she?

Dreams don't come true. Life had taught her that lesson more than once.

Ignoring the voice in her head, Anna badgered, "C'mon, Leon, Ryan must have said *something* about himself."

"He's not much of a talker."

"You mean Ryan was unsociable? Rude?"

"No. Just quiet."

"He doesn't appreciate us, does he?"

"Leave him be, Anna. If he don't want to fit in around here, he don't have to."

"But I wanted—"

"Everyone to get along." *Slurp.* "Always watching out for the strays, aren't you?" Leon shoved his chair back, but Anna pressed her hand against his shoulder.

"Keep the ice on your knees." She grabbed the coffeepot and topped off his cup, then added a dollop of nonfat dairy creamer.

"A man can't even enjoy a coffee with real cream," he complained.

After Leon was diagnosed with high cholesterol a year ago, Leon's wife had enlisted Anna's aid in monitoring her husband's fat intake at work. "Helga would have my head if I let you have real cream."

"Helga should pick on someone her own size." Leon grinned and Anna laughed. Two inches shorter than Anna, his wife weighed in at a whopping one hundred eighty. And Leon was hopelessly in love with every one of those pounds. Sometimes Anna wondered if she'd ever find a man who'd love her to distraction the way Leon loved Helga.

Leon scratched the top of his bald noggin. "Jones mentioned he was divorced."

"Oh." Not sure why the news unsettled her, she asked, "Any children?" Before Leon answered, the bell in the office jangled. "Probably Bobby." Anna was halfway across the room when the door flew open.

Ryan froze midstride, mouth tight at the corners. His habit of scowling when their gazes connected annoyed Anna. Didn't he realize a person used more facial muscles to frown than to smile?

Feeling mischievous, she flashed a wide grin. "Hello, Ryan. Forget your lunch box?" *Or your manners, perhaps?*

Shifting his scowl to Leon and then back to Anna, he muttered, "I walked off with these." He held out a pair of work gloves. An oil smudge marked the side of his jaw. A tree twig poked out of the top of his mussed hair and flecks of dirt dusted his cheeks and nose.

Her attention bounced between the gloves and the lines of exhaustion etched in his face. His cranky expression prevented her from offering one of her special sympathy hugs.

A throat cleared. "Think I'll head home." Leon placed his mug in the sink, grabbed his lunch box and nodded goodbye on his way out.

The faint trace of Ryan's aftershave drifted beneath Anna's big nose. She hated everything about her nose except one thing—it was a good sniffer. Mixed with the sexy, sophisticated scent of Ryan's cologne was the tang of sweat and hardworking male. An odor her nose insisted wasn't unappealing.

"You could have brought in the gloves tomorrow."

Ryan's plan to sneak in and out of the station without anyone the wiser had bombed big-time. He cursed himself for wanting to return the gloves when he could have stuffed them into a mailing envelope, instead.

"Are you feeling all right?" The touch of her feminine hand on his arm made his flesh prickle.

"I'm fine." What the hell was wrong with him? He'd known women more beautiful than Anna and hadn't reacted physically to them. *That was before 9/11. Before you crawled into your cave and swore off the opposite sex.* What could he say other than the truth—he'd returned the gloves because he had no intention of showing up for work tomorrow. He tossed the gloves onto the table, then stuffed his hands into the front pockets of his jeans, where they wouldn't be tempted to finger the blond hair that feathered across Anna's forehead.

"Did anything happen this afternoon?" she inquired.

Yeah. You happened—Ms. Anastazia Persistence Nowakowski.

When her gaze softened with concern, he battled the urge to confide in her—as if a mere stranger could make sense of the feelings at war within him. He'd arrived at the station this morning, ready to do his grandfather's bidding, prepared to feel uncomfortable working with strangers. But he hadn't anticipated being blindsided by Anna. By her perpetually happy demeanor. By her compelling face. By her nonstop chatter.

She irritated the hell out of him.

He wasn't angry with her for awakening his long-dead libido. He was angry because he sensed something about her…something that warned him that if he wasn't careful she'd worm her way inside him to the place he'd promised he'd never, ever allow another woman access to.

The best way to prevent that from happening was to keep his distance. And Anna was the kind of woman who stepped over boundaries. Knocked down Do Not Enter signposts. And ripped up Keep Out posters. He had no choice but to quit.

"Ryan?"

"Everything's fine." Or would be as soon as he got the hell out.

"Oh, good."

At her relieved smile, his chest expanded with gentle yearning. Anna was full of life, compassion and caring. And he was full of...*nothing*.

"You'd tell me if a problem surfaced, wouldn't you?" She fluttered a hand in front of her face. "If I can't fix it, then Bobby will." She moved to the counter. "Let me get you a cup of coffee."

"Stop." He cringed at her round-eyed expression. He hadn't meant to shout the word. "No coffee." He wanted away from her smile. Away from her kindness. Away from *her*.

"Hate to waste the last cup." Against his wishes, she poured the coffee and delivered the mug to the table. "Might as well sit a spell and wait out rush hour before heading home," she coaxed.

Annoyed with himself for giving in, he joined her and grunted. "Shouldn't you be heading home to your own family?" *Damn*. Now she'd assume he was fishing for details about her personal life. He wasn't. For all he cared, she could be married, single, divorced, a lesbian or all of the above.

"I'm single."

Was it his imagination, or did her smile tremble with strain? He sipped the too-hot brew to keep from asking *why* she wasn't married.

"My roommate is a student at the Culinary Academy

of New York and rarely arrives at our apartment before seven each night."

As if cooking school explained why she'd never married.

Anna traced a scratch in the Formica table with the tip of her pink nail. "How did things go with Mr. Kline's house?"

What would a ten-minute tête-à-tête hurt when he'd never see her again? "We cleared everything out except for the bathroom toilets, sinks and the tub."

"Eryk doubles as a plumber. He'll have everything disconnected and ready to rip out in no time. His rates are reasonable, especially for friends."

After eight hours on the job, she assumed Ryan and the other men were friends?

"Next week you'll be working with Antonio and Joe on the lot-cleanup program."

Silence stretched between them. God, he was rusty at mundane dialogue. Her gaze skirted his face, then she stared him in the eye. "You don't like it here, do you?"

Ms. Chatterbox could read minds. He wasn't certain how to respond—not that words mattered. She offered no chance to defend himself.

"Have I insulted you?" Her chin lifted. Sparks spit from her eyes, heightening the blue color. A rosy tinge seeped across her cheekbones, making her nose more pronounced. Her expressive face captivated him.

Ryan's ex-wife had taken great pains to control her emotions—until she'd visited him in the hospital after 9/11. For the first time her carefully schooled features gave way to disgust. Revulsion. Pity. Perfect Sandra had discovered she had an imperfect husband.

"Are you angry at one of the guys?"

"No." Leon and Eryk were decent men and once they'd figured out Ryan wasn't verbose, they'd left him alone.

"Then you're always this social and outgoing?" The corner of her mouth twitched.

Anastazia Nowakowski was a piece of work. "More or less." He fought an answering smile.

"You won't object if I work on your *demeanor* while you're employed at Parnell Brothers?"

The last thing he needed was to be this woman's pet project. Cause. Or charity case. His decision to quit hadn't been made lightly. He understood he'd lose his inheritance and that his grandfather wouldn't approve, especially after his brothers had stuck out their life lessons. But right now he'd rather face an irate old man than the big-as-saucers blue eyes across the table.

Her earnest expression pulled at him. When was the last time a woman had gazed at him the way Anna Nowakowski watched him now—as if *he* held her happiness in the palm of his hand. Would it hurt to hang around the job awhile longer?

"Don't worry, I'll play nice." Her lips spread into a wide grin. "You'll be best buddies with your coworkers in no time."

Don't get your hopes up, Ms. Sunshine.

Anna was an intelligent girl. From what he'd witnessed, she practically ran the business. After a few failed attempts to lure him into the fold, she'd give up and leave him be. "Do you ever stop smiling?" he groused.

The sound of her lilting laughter soothed his apprehension.

"Better keep on your toes, Ryan Jones. If I have my way, you'll be the one smiling all the time."

Chapter Three

"TGIF!" Eryk hollered over his shoulder.

Following at a distance, Ryan noted that Leon waited in the driver's seat of the dump truck. Why the hurry to return to the station for lunch?

Ryan hopped into the truck, his lower-back muscles protesting—one too many swings with a sledgehammer. He'd reconciled himself to remaining in a state of perpetual exhaustion for the duration of the week. Add in the mental and emotional stress of Ms. Happy Chatty's isn't-the-world-a-beautiful-place smile, and then expending precious energy avoiding her nonstop attempts to drag him into discussions with the men, was it any wonder he teetered on the verge of collapse?

"What do you guess she made for the potluck?" Eryk grabbed the dashboard when Leon veered right out of the south Queens neighborhood of Lindenwood.

Potluck. Ryan shuddered. Anna had informed him several times about the once-a-month potluck. When he'd discovered the teddy-bear-shaped sticky note on his locker reminding him to bring cookies, he'd suffered a full-blown panic attack. Feeling like the potluck grinch, he'd brought a sack lunch and intended to eat outside on the stoop *alone*—the same as every other day this week.

Until Eryk had knocked on the Porta Potti yesterday while Ryan had been inside, Ryan hadn't considered how much he appreciated working in his office isolated from his employees. Over the past six years his direct contact with people had decreased, until weeks passed before he spoke face-to-face with another human.

"Maybe Anna brought Blair's famous spicy sausage-stuffed mushrooms," Leon said, answering Eryk's earlier question. A minute later, Leon steered the truck into the station garage and cut the engine.

Ryan didn't care who Blair was. They piled out of the truck, and the scent of garlic bread overpowered the usual smell of diesel fuel and engine grease. He followed the others to the break room, his stomach rumbling at the mouthwatering aroma.

"'Bout time you fellas showed up." Patrick scooped spoonfuls of Italian casserole onto a plastic plate. Antonio, Joe and the company boss, Bobby, stuffed their faces at the table covered with an American-flag cloth.

"Everything looks real nice, Anna," Eryk complimented her, then moved to the sink to wash up.

Nice? The Fourth of July had exploded in the room. Coordinated red-white-and-blue plates and utensils rested on the counter. Two pitchers of lemonade with real lemon slices floating on the top occupied the middle of the table. Anna had tied red-and-blue balloons to the chairs and stuck American-flag toothpicks in the brownies stacked on a plate. The one thing missing— real fireworks.

"I wanted to use the leftover party supplies from our Fourth of July picnic." Anna glanced at Ryan, but he ducked his head, grabbed his lunch from the fridge and slipped through the door that led to the lockers, where Leon was changing into a clean T-shirt. When he noticed Ryan's sack lunch, he frowned.

"Don't have much of an appetite," Ryan mumbled, attempting to escape.

Leon blocked his path. "You just unfriendly or has one of us offended?"

Well, hell. He should have assumed sneaking off wouldn't be easy. "I'm not feeling well and I was searching for peace and quiet." The fib wasn't far from the truth. People made his stomach queasy.

"Anna's got over-the-counter medicine—"

"No, thanks."

The skin on the top of Leon's bald head wrinkled.

Before the other man had the chance to argue further, Ryan hustled out of the locker room, cut through the garage and managed to scamper up the steps to the office door without being stopped. Appetite gone, he tossed the lunch bag aside, collapsed on the cold concrete stoop, rested his arms on his knees and buried his head in his hands.

When had his desire to be alone changed from a preference to a gut-gnawing need? Had his grandfather noticed Ryan's obsession with isolation had evolved into a phobia? Had Ryan tricked himself into believing he could manage the bouts of panic he experienced around other people?

Just how screwed up am I?

The muted sounds of male laughter echoed through the garage. A fierce, steal-his-breath pang of loneliness seized him. The worker's camaraderie conjured up memories of his brothers and him at their grandfather's home on Martha's Vineyard. Afternoons filled with laughter and arguments. But always togetherness.

Even after Ryan had married he'd managed to hang out with his brothers a few times a year. After 9/11, he'd forced himself to visit Aaron and Nelson, but not as often, and their relationship had never been the same.

Who's fault is that?

What did it matter? Both his brothers were happily married, busy with their families. Ryan missed them. Missed his old life. Missed his old self. Plain damn *missed*.

"I brought you dessert." Anna stood at the bottom of the steps holding a napkin-wrapped brownie—*not* smiling.

Her solemn gaze bore into him. Could she see into his soul? Smell his fear? As much as he hated her constant smile, he didn't wish to be the reason for her frown.

"Thanks," he managed, accepting the treat.

She eyed his lunch sack. "Leon said you weren't feeling well."

"Queasy stomach." Embarrassed at the raspy note in his voice, he pretended interest in the line of cars waiting for a green light a block away.

"Mind if I join you?" In Anna-like fashion she didn't wait for an invitation. She claimed the third step, her shoulder even with his knee.

Ryan braced himself for the surge of panic he anticipated at her closeness. Seconds ticked by and…*nothing*. He studied her profile—the bump along the bridge of her nose barely visible from this angle. Her pale skin—poreless smooth porcelain. Flawless. His fingers ached to touch the unblemished perfection.

A scent—sweet and fruity—drifted up his nostrils. He breathed deeply, this time detecting a hint of Anna's unique feminine scent. The sudden twitch in his pants caught him by surprise and he shifted away.

"The first aid kit contains—"

"I'm fine." He cursed himself for lying to Leon. Fibbing had become an integral part of his everyday life. *I'm fine. No, nothing's wrong. Everything's great.* Untruths that allowed him to keep others at a distance. Hell, he even lied to himself so he wouldn't analyze his every thought and emotion. Believing he was empty inside made life bearable.

ANNA TWISTED on the step in order to make eye contact. Growing up in foster care had taught her to read other people. In some cases it had been a matter of survival— hers. Her intuition insisted the pain reflected on Ryan's face went deeper than a sour stomach. "If you didn't want to participate in the potluck, all you had to do was say so."

His stony face reminded her of a solemn boy in one of her foster homes. With haunted eyes, the silent six-year-old had spied on the foster parents from corners and stairwells—never speaking. His moodiness had frightened the adults and they'd exchanged him for a child who *worked.*

Troubled by her foster parents' actions, eight-year-old Anna had transformed herself into a cheery, happy, never-complaining child. In the end her efforts had fallen short. Without understanding why, she'd been removed from the home and placed elsewhere. She'd tried harder…and harder and harder each time she'd landed in a new home. Years of cheerful conditioning had had a lasting effect on her. It simply took too much effort to be a grump. Nevertheless, Ryan's perpetually ornery mood had taken a toll on her internal happy meter.

Anna wasn't sure why Ryan's moodiness bothered her. Or why it mattered that he preferred to be left alone. She thought of her daughter, Tina. Almost eighteen years had passed since she had allowed her baby to be adopted. Anna's heart ached at the possibility her daughter had grown up to be a Ryan Jones—a solitary soul surrounded by people but alone in the world.

"I'm sorry," he blurted, interrupting her contemplation.

"Sorry for what?"

"Sorry I didn't bring cookies for the potluck."

His hangdog expression made her smile.

"What's so funny?" he grumbled.

"Nothing." He opened his mouth, but she cut him off. "I came out here to tell you that after our potluck lunches, I give haircuts to the guys."

"Haircuts?"

One would think an uptown guy would be able to articulate more than one-word utterances. "I was a hairdresser before I hired on here."

"What do you charge?"

Wow, a full sentence. "Whatever you can afford to put in the tip jar. I donate the money to a children's after-school program in the neighborhood." When Ryan didn't respond, she hinted, "You could use a trim." Anna wondered if her interest in him was motivated by concern or attraction. A little of both, she suspected. She stood and brushed off the seat of her jeans, aware his eyes followed the swish-swash of her fingers against her bottom.

Ryan Jones was a sexy, attractive, edgy guy. A man she definitely wanted to learn more about. "I'll be in the locker room if you change your mind about a haircut...." *Or me.*

"WALK THE LOT and search for any surprises left overnight," Bobby Parnell instructed Ryan as he parked the company vehicle on a side street in the Elmhurst area of Queens. "I'll help the guys unload the excavator." The boss slid from the driver's seat and headed for Antonio's Ford F-250, which had been used to tow the miniexcavator.

Ryan went in the opposite direction. The cleanup project he'd been assigned his second week on the job consisted of three lots sandwiched between two apartment buildings. Monday, they'd gotten rid of old appliances, tires, trash and broken furniture. Tuesday, they'd demolished the remainder of a crumbling brick mom-and-pop grocery that had been vacant for years. Wednesday—today—would be spent transporting debris to the dump, then using the excavator to break up the old concrete. Tomorrow, Leon and Eryk would join the group with the second dump truck and haul away the rubble.

As he canvassed the area, Ryan struggled to envision the final transformation—a neighborhood community center.

"Find anything?" Joe joined Ryan in the far corner of the lot.

"Nope."

Shielding his eyes from the sun, Joe pointed to the apartments across the street. "Damn gangs."

Earlier in the week Ryan had noticed the colorful images painted on the west side of the building. He didn't condone defacing property, but the mural was a nice piece of work. The punk artist should put his talent to better use. "I heard your brother's involved in a gang."

"You heard about Willie?" Before Ryan answered, Joe added, "Anna told you."

"She mentioned you were concerned about your brother."

"He's fifteen and full of himself. Thinks he can walk away from the gang anytime he wants."

After following in his elder brother, Nelson's, footsteps and graduating from Harvard, Ryan had moved to New York City and had lived there ever since, but he confessed he was ignorant of the struggles facing the four boroughs outside Manhattan. "Are you implying the group won't let him leave?"

The hollow sound of Joe's laugh drifted across the lot. "The only way out of a gang is in a body bag."

"What kind of trouble does the gang cause?" Ryan chose to believe his inquisitiveness was the result of his acclimation to interacting with the guys and not because of a sense of connection he'd developed with them.

"The gang's idea of fun is to barge into baptisms and weddings, threaten the guests, then steal the alcohol." Joe rolled a chunk of concrete under his work boot.

"Fun at the expense of others."

"Yep. The group thrives on shoplifting, selling fake green cards, dealing drugs and extorting small-business owners. You know what pisses me off most?" The younger man vented as if he believed his coworker cared.

And surprisingly, Ryan did. "What?"

"Willie's got people who care about him. A decent home. Parents who love him. He doesn't fit the profile of a gangbanger. He's not a runaway and he hasn't been abandoned or abused by his parents."

The next time Ryan spoke with his grandfather he'd remind the old man how fortunate he was that none of his

grandsons had taken to a life of crime. Although he suspected his grandfather might argue that he'd have preferred managing a recalcitrant teenager than doling out life
lessons to grown men. "If your brother has a lot of time
on his hands, what about encouraging him to get a job?"

Joe gaped. "He can make more money protecting
prostitutes than flipping burgers." With a snort of
disgust, he added, "It doesn't matter."

"What doesn't matter?"

"If Willie leaves the gang, they'll put a bounty on his
head."

A bounty? The scenario had the makings of a Hol-
lywood movie. "What about asking the police for
protection?"

"They'd don't care. They'd just as soon let all the
gangs kill each other off and be rid of the problem."

Frustration steamed from the top of Joe's head. Had
Ryan's grandfather experienced this same helplessness
when Ryan had determinedly walled himself off from
the family after 9/11?

"All we can do is wait," Joe mumbled. "Wait for my
brother's luck to run out."

An image of the man's family, gathered around a
headstone in a cemetery, swept through Ryan's mind.
He had to help. *This is none of your business. Keep
your mouth shut.* "Maybe I—"

"C'mon," Joe interrupted. "The boss is waving us over."

What had gotten into Ryan? If not for the boss's
timely interruption he'd have… *What?* Offered to save
Willie? Hadn't 9/11 taught him the danger of rescuing
people? He'd tossed out his superhero duds a long time
ago. No more surrendering himself for someone else—
besides, he didn't have anything left *to* sacrifice. He had

enough of his own problems—mainly why he had no trouble conversing with the guys, but when it came to talking with Anna, he froze inside.

That's because she unnerves you.

At times Ryan suspected her blue eyes could see his deepest secrets. Deepest fears. After his near slipup with Joe a few moments ago, he'd best keep his distance from Anna. That shouldn't be difficult.

She was a female. And females were so far down on his list they weren't even on the paper.

"HI, EVERYONE!" Anna waved as she shut the door of the boss's pickup she'd driven to the work site. Since the men were stuck in Elmhurst, she decided to bring Ryan's birthday party to the crew. Leaving the cake on the front seat, she approached Bobby, who watched Joe break up concrete with the bulldozer. Antonio, Ryan and Eryk were tossing debris into the dump trucks, while Leon used a minibackhoe to deposit the larger chunks. "Can you take a break?" she shouted above the grinding gears of machines.

"What for?" Bobby hollered.

"Birthday cake."

"Well, heck, Anna. Why didn't you say so in the first place?" Bobby possessed a mean sweet tooth.

The chugging noise of motors filled the air as she rested the two-tiered confection on the hood of the truck. She removed the plastic wrap protecting the white-frosting swirls. Her roommate, Blair, had baked the chocolate cake, but she'd stayed up half the night decorating the layers.

"Hey, whose birthday is it?" Antonio peered over Anna's shoulder.

Smile in place, she faced the men assembled around her. "Ryan's." As was his custom, the birthday boy remained a respectable distance from the group. She looked him in the eye and he took her by surprise when he *didn't* glance away. She wished he had. His glower insisted he wasn't pleased with the surprise party. *Oh dear.*

Pasting on a happy face, she spouted, "Ryan's thirty-seven today."

A barrage of old-age jokes followed her pronouncement, none of which made a crack in Ryan's stone face. Anna glanced longingly at the box of candles on the front seat. By the time they coaxed Ryan to blow them out, the cake would catch fire.

She reached for the knife, but Joe cried, "Wait. We have to sing 'Happy Birthday.'"

"Maybe Patrick would lead us?" Anna offered the shy man an encouraging smile. After a few seconds, raucous male bellowing drowned out Patrick's beautiful voice. To keep from bursting into laughter at Ryan's horrified expression, Anna locked her gaze on the bulldozer.

As the last notes of the song faded, she clapped her hands. Then, amid murmurs of appreciation, she served the cake, handing Ryan the largest piece. "Happy Birthday."

"Thanks." As if a pistol were being held to his head, he shoveled a bite into his mouth.

"Good, huh?" Antonio mumbled, cheeks bulging.

"Yeah, great." Ryan's glare pierced Anna.

For the life of her, she couldn't understand what she'd done to annoy him. There was only one explanation for his pathetic lack of appreciation for her thoughtfulness—he didn't care for her. And that hurt.

Everyone was fond of her. She worked darn hard to guarantee no one found fault with her. Ticked, she said, "Seconds, Ryan?"

He shook his head, then placed the remainder of his cake—the entire piece minus one bite—on the hood.

"I'll wrap the cake for you to take home."

"No," he blurted, then lowered his voice. "I'm not fond of sweets. The guys can share the rest of it."

Anna couldn't explain what sparked her anger—the fact that Ryan didn't appreciate her attempt to make his birthday special or that she'd permitted his rudeness to hurt her. And the reason his rudeness could hurt her, she decided, was that she'd allowed herself to care about him.

Stupid, Anna. Ever since you offered your baby up for adoption, you've tried to mother everyone and anyone. Well, Ryan Jones doesn't need or want a mother. She lifted the entire cake from the hood and held it out to him. "Take it. After all, it's your birthday."

He raised his hands. "I don't want it."

Uncaring that the rest of the guys had stopped eating to gawk at her and Ryan, she stepped closer and insisted, "You're being too generous."

"No, I'm not." He retreated.

Anna advanced a step. "Yes." And another. "You." Another. "Are."

Hell. Anastazia Nowakowski didn't recognize when to give up. Backed into a corner, Ryan decided he'd better accept the cake before the happy-birthday-girl shoved it in his face.

Anna's blue eyes sparkled with… *Tears?* "You're welcome." She spun away.

While the guys thanked her, Ryan stood aside cursing himself for being such a bastard and wounding her feelings.

How could Anna have known he'd stopped celebrating birthdays and holidays the moment he learned his ex-wife had miscarried their child?

Chapter Four

I'm sorry.

Ryan paced in front of Anna's desk, rehearsing an apology in his head. Hoping to make amends for his rude reaction to her surprise birthday celebration that afternoon, he'd hung around the locker room until the men had left the building. The *click-click* of Anna's heels announced her arrival seconds before she appeared in the doorway.

When she spotted him, she paused, one sandaled foot hovering an inch above the floor. Her mouth flattened into a thin line and the light dimmed in her normally sparkling eyes. After a moment, she unpaused, moved into the room and sat in the chair at her desk.

No hello. No get out of here. No nothing.

"Got a minute, Anna?"

A shoulder shrug. Averting her gaze, she shuffled papers. Stacked and restacked folders. Tightened the lid on her correction-fluid bottle. Loaded staples into the stapler. He got the hint. She didn't care to listen to anything he had to say.

Edging closer to the desk, he positioned himself in her line of vision. She vacated the chair, crossed the

room to the water stand and filled her coffee mug, then
gave the hanging plants by the front window a drink. He
tried again. "Please, Anna." God, he hoped she wouldn't
make him beg.

Long, slim, pink-tipped fingers clenched the kitten
photo on the ceramic mug. Then she faced him—chin
out and with an I-won't-let-you-hurt-me glare.

"I was an ass."

Her eyes narrowed to slits, the blue barely visible.

He'd already admitted he'd been a jerk. What more
did she want—blood? "About the birthday cake... I
apologize for hurting your feelings."

The slits widened.

Hell. He shouldn't have used that stupid word—
feelings. Women loved examining them. Dissecting
them. Declaring them. He'd learned from his ex-wife
that whenever the word *feeling* entered a heart-to-heart,
ninety-five percent of the time he'd never said what
she'd wanted to hear.

"I didn't mean to be rude." He waited for "That's
okay" or "No harm done."

He got, "You hurt my feelings."

That damn word again. "I'd like to make amends."

"Okay. Buy me a cup of coffee."

"Coffee?" Couldn't he say he was sorry again? Did
he have to spend time with her?

"The Muddy River Café is a few blocks from here."
She retrieved her sweater from the desk chair, then slung
her purse strap over her shoulder.

While she locked up, he struggled to figure out how
I'm sorry had evolved into *let me buy you a coffee.*

Side by side they strolled in silence, casting glances
in each other's direction. They rounded a corner and

stumbled upon a group of teens roughhousing in front of a dry-cleaning business. Automatically, Ryan placed his hand on Anna's back and put himself between her and the kids as they passed. Not until the end of the fourth block did he realize that his hand lingered on Anna. How long had it been since he'd pressed his palm to a feminine curve?

You need to get laid.

If he wanted sex, he could find a woman to scratch his itch. But 9/11 and his divorce had worn him out physically, mentally and emotionally. As a survivor of the terrorist attack, he understood on some level that he harbored a desperate desire to connect with another human being. The *desperation* aspect scared him away from personal entanglements. If the relationship bombed, he'd be worse off than he was right now— hollow inside.

When and if he decided to make love to a woman, it wouldn't be with one who pitied him. And once Anna saw his body, she'd pity him. She wouldn't mean to. But he suspected pity came naturally to a person with as big a heart as Anna possessed.

At the next corner they stopped to wait for the cross-walk light and he forced himself to remove his hand from her back.

"Why?"

"Why what?" he blurted, caught off guard by her question.

"It was just a birthday cake, Ryan. Your reaction was over the top. I deserve an explanation."

The fact that she was right didn't make explaining easier. He was saved from answering when the light switched to green. Grasping her elbow, he guided her across the intersection and into the café. The place was crowded and loud and Ryan hated it immediately.

Groups of gossiping women, giggling teens too young to be coffee addicts, slouched in big comfortable chairs and slurped from their cups. The stools at the counter were occupied, and a line formed at the register. He intended to suggest they buy their coffee at the doughnut shop they'd passed along the way, but Anna had already secured a spot in the order line. He noticed an older couple vacate a table near the front window. "I'll get the coffee. You grab that table."

"Black, no sugar, no cream."

A no-nonsense coffee for a no-nonsense woman. Anna wove a path through the crowd and Ryan wondered if she was aware of the appreciative glances that followed the swish-sway of her curvy backside. When she reached the table, she turned her chair toward the other patrons. He'd never met a person who wished to be with people more than Anna. He suspected it didn't matter if they were friend, foe or stranger as long as they kept her company.

Anna twisted sideways to drape her sweater over the chair. The action pulled her silk blouse across her generous breasts. The part of his body that generally hovered near zero suddenly warmed and he forced his attention back to the menu on the wall. Anna was a pretty woman with a Marilyn Monroe body. Dangerous and intriguing, she scared the hell out of him.

He had no intention of allowing his male appreciation to advance further than ogling. Becoming intimate with Anna would mean opening himself up emotionally. No way did Ryan wish for Ms. Happy Chatty to see through him to the dark side of his soul—his lost hopes, lost joys, lost self.

Out of the corner of his eye he watched a man approach Anna. She popped off the chair and hugged him as if he were her favorite teddy bear. Then she invited the guy to sit—in *his* chair. An old friend? Maybe a lover? Hell, Anna probably hugged all her acquaintances.

Next in line, Ryan rattled off his order. Less than a minute later, coffee cups in hand, he approached the cozy couple. Deep in discussion, neither acknowledged his presence until he cleared his throat.

"Ryan." Anna accepted her drink from him and motioned to her friend. "This is Charlie. Charlie…meet Ryan."

"How do you do." Charlie stood and offered his hand. "Anna and I go way back."

In years or bed? He shook hands, adding a bit of *oomph* to his grip.

"Grab a chair and visit awhile longer, Charlie," Anna suggested.

The man ruffled her hair. "I should get going, brat."

Brat? Now Ryan was intrigued. What kind of relationship did the two have?

Anna bumped Ryan out of the way and hugged Charlie. *Again.* "Say hi to Alice and the kids."

The guy's married. A zing of what could be labeled relief shot through him. Ryan and Charlie exchanged manly nods, then the guy left.

The longest minute of Ryan's life passed before Anna smiled and asked, "Aren't you curious about Charlie?"

God, yes. He studied his cup and muttered, "He's none of my business."

"You're a private person." Anna was careful with her words.

His family had never used the word *private* to describe his need to be left alone. "I'm not very social." Part truth. Before 9/11 he'd been considered a fun guy.

"Thank you for the coffee." Her smile was half the wattage of the one she'd bestowed upon her pal Charlie.

"Do you come here often?" He faced his chair to the window.

"No. There's another Muddy River near my apartment." She tilted her head and narrowed her eyes. "You don't cater to crowds, either."

Intuitive little brat. He slouched, attempting to convey an air of nonchalance, when in reality his body was coiled as tight as a roll of electrical wire. "Not especially."

"Why?"

Couldn't this woman stay on her side of the fence? He imagined she was the kind of neighbor who waved while a man was mowing the lawn and kept waving until he turned off the mower, walked across the yard and asked what she wanted, to which she'd reply, "Oh, nothing. Just saying hello."

He swallowed a gulp of coffee, ignoring the sear of heat against his throat. "Long work hours and socializing don't mix."

"Liar."

Man, her eyes got to him. Bright. Blue. Animated. "What did you call me?" He was having a hell of a time keeping track of the argument.

"I called you a liar. You avoid people because you're afraid not because you're too busy."

So much for keeping his soul hidden. "Not everyone is a people person like you, Anna."

The light in her eyes dimmed. "Being friendly isn't easy for me. I've worked at it all my life."

Was she joking? "Well, practice makes perfect. The guys at the station believe you walk on water."

"We're like family."

"How long have you worked for Parnell?"

"Ten years. I turned twenty-two right after I hired on."

"You got the job right out of college?"

"I didn't go to college. I went to beauty school, and at the time I was working in a hair salon and not liking the long hours, little pay and achy legs."

"Then why did you go to beauty school?"

She shrugged. "I was told it was the best a girl in my situation could hope for."

"Your situation?" Their chat had evolved into a game of twenty questions.

"My last set of foster parents convinced me that cutting hair was a decent, respectable occupation for a young woman of no means."

Anna had grown up in the foster-care system? At least he'd had his brothers and his grandfather after his parents had passed away. "What happened to your family?"

"My mother died when I was four. I never knew my father. His name wasn't on my birth certificate."

He envisioned a four-year-old with humongous blue eyes, standing on a stranger's doorstep. "I'm sorry."

"I was lucky, I suppose, to survive foster care relatively unscathed." She gazed unseeingly across the café, a pinched expression on her face, as if she was reliving an unpleasant memory.

The thought of Anna as a small child afraid or threatened shook Ryan in a way that not even he understood. "You've had a rough life."

"Life is what you make of it."

For a moment he considered her words, then shoved

them aside. He wasn't in the mood for the old if-life-hands-you-lemons-make-lemonade speech. Besides, they'd digressed from the purpose of their coffee outing. "Are you going to accept my apology?"

"Of course."

That's it? "You don't want me to grovel?"

"No. I should apologize for bullying you in front of the men. I don't usually lose my temper."

His hand found hers across the tabletop and squeezed. "Don't make excuses for me." He had a hunch she justified everyone's wrongdoing in order to keep the seas of her world calm and waveless. "I was an idiot. I'm sorry, and—" he persisted when she opened her mouth to protest "—you deserve an explanation."

A tilt of her head sent her blond locks cascading over one shoulder. "I'm listening."

"I haven't celebrated my birthday in a long time. I don't even open the cards my brothers and grandfather send." He paused, expecting a reaction. Instead, she waited patiently for him to finish. "I stopped celebrating my birthday and other holidays after my ex-wife miscarried."

Anna's curious expression froze, the blood draining from her face, leaving her as pale as if she'd walked across a grave.

"I'm sorry, Ryan." The words, barely audible, slipped out between unmoving lips.

"It was a long time ago," he said, attempting to comfort her. Anna's bleached-flour complexion remained. "Finish with your coffee."

She did, but whatever had troubled her hovered in the air. He braced for other questions: *How long were you married? Did you and your wife have other children?*

Her attention remained riveted on life outside the window, and the questions remained unspoken. Seconds turned into minutes, then she stood. "Let's go."

Unconcerned he might appear eager to end their evening, Ryan sprang to his feet. On the way out, he deposited their empty cups in the trash receptacle by the door.

A gust of cool air greeted them outside. Anna drew her sweater on. Part of Ryan craved to snuggle her and promise to defend her against whatever had troubled her earlier. The other part begged to run the opposite way and pretend he hadn't noticed her traumatic reaction.

Lest he make a monster-size mistake, he shoved his hands into the front pockets of his jeans and strolled beside her. After a block, she glanced up and smiled. This was the Anna she intended people to see—confident, friendly, full of life. The pain in her eyes gone now, replaced by a glimmer of wary warmth.

Everyone had fears and needs. So what was it about Anna that made Ryan yearn to slay her dragons? Made him believe he was capable of helping her, when his own life was so screwed up? If 9/11 had taught him anything, it was that life went on—for everyone else but him.

An image of his empty, silent apartment flashed through his mind and his steps slowed. "Where do you live? I'll walk you home."

NOT TONIGHT, Anna thought. "My apartment is in Ridgewood." She checked her watch, then picked up the pace. "If I hurry, I can catch the 6:35 bus."

Maybe he'd take the hint and veer off at the corner. The news of Ryan's ex-wife's miscarriage had stunned her. Yes, she felt horrible that he'd suffered the loss of a child, but it was the look in his eyes that had cut her off at the knees. *Pain.* Sharp and deep. Without a word, he'd conveyed his agony at not being able to save his child. That the fate of his own flesh and blood had been taken from his hands.

She knew a little about fate and being its victim. She'd lost a child, too. Forced to give up her baby for adoption by social services, she'd experienced anger, resentment, hurt and loneliness. But she'd been spared the one misery Ryan hadn't—her baby had lived.

Although she harbored tremendous guilt and sorrow. Deep in her heart she believed she would have been a good mother. If someone had been around to help her raise her child… But there had been no one. She remembered thinking that her baby had been lucky. A family had welcomed her, unlike the baby's mother, whom no one had wanted.

At fourteen, scared and alone, she'd done what she'd thought best.

Now she understood why she'd been attracted to Ryan from the very beginning. Aside from his good looks and brooding personality, they'd connected with each other on an unconscious level, each having experienced the loss of a child. Sadness swelled inside Anna, until she thought she'd choke on the emotion. Ryan had been the first man in forever to intrigue her, challenge her and attract her. And now no chance of anything but a strained friendship could develop between them, because Ryan would never understand why she'd given her baby up for adoption.

How funny that she'd been the one to pester and cajole him into opening up and socializing with her and the other men at the station. And just when he'd shown signs of emerging from his shell, she was scurrying back into hers.

"I'll see you to the bus stop." Ryan grasped her elbow.

The simple courtesy stung Anna's eyes and she muttered, "When you apologize, you go all the way."

He chuckled—a full, throaty sound that sent shivers scurrying across her skin. The man's charm was lethal. "I take the train most days. Do you ride the bus to work every day?"

Good. A nice, safe, nonemotional dialogue about mass transit. "Yep. I don't own a car so I get around by bus or train."

"No car?"

She didn't understand why he sounded surprised. Thousands of people in NYC didn't own automobiles.

"I have an underground parking space at my apartment," he added.

Lucky him. Her brownstone didn't have a garage. But she had a basement, which she used for storage, and a washer and dryer.

Two blocks down, three to go. "What do you think of the job so far?"

He rolled his shoulders.

"Does that mean better than you'd expected or worse?" She waited for him to elaborate. When he didn't, she suspected he preferred more intellectually stimulating work. "Are you becoming more comfortable around the guys?"

"Joe mentioned his brother, Willie."

Surprised Joe had brought up Willie, she murmured, "The teen's criminal activity has been tough on his family."

"Joe explained that even if his brother decided to leave the gang, he can't."

"I'm certain Willie wishes he'd never begun hanging around those losers in the first place."

"What do the authorities suggest in cases such as this?"

"If Willie agrees to be a snitch, the police will offer protection, or so they claim. We've all heard stories of snitches being assassinated under the watchful eyes of the cops. Joe worries about the rest of the family. Gangs target family members when they discover they've been betrayed."

"Why doesn't Joe move his family out of the area?"

Ryan's interest in his coworker's dilemma was at odds with his usual gruff, distant demeanor. She might have found that unusual if not for catching a glimpse of the man beneath the mask a short time ago. That he was affected by the loss of an unborn child convinced Anna that Ryan suffered deeply.

"Leaving isn't that simple. Joe's father has been on disability for a while now and his doctors are here. His mother has taught Sunday school for fifteen years at their church and every Christmas she sews the costumes for the holiday play. And all their relatives live in the area. Pulling up roots and moving somewhere new isn't an option."

They walked the last block to the bus stop in silence. Anna expected Ryan to wave and go on. Instead, he waited by her side. The heat in his eyes made her self-conscious. She rubbed her nose.

"It's perfect," he said.

"What's perfect?"

"Your nose. It's just right for your face."

Oh. My. God. Had she spoken her thoughts? Her neck heated, but she resisted the urge to turn away. "Yeah, well, how would you enjoy walking around with a sniffer the size of a Polish pickle?"

"Speaking of pickles, are you Polish?"

"Does Nowakowski sound English to you?"

He grinned. She could get used to his sexy smile. "I'm mostly Irish. Black Irish," he added.

She'd never heard of Jones being an Irish name. "When I think of Irish, I picture red hair, freckles, leprechauns and pots of gold."

Talk ceased as the bus crept along the curb and belched black exhaust from its tailpipe like a big nasty fart. "Thanks for the coffee and the conversation." When she moved to join the throng of people boarding, Ryan snagged an arm.

"Anna." His eyes flashed, but silence followed her name. Finally he released her. She boarded the bus, scanned her Metro Card, then located a seat in the rear. As the bus pulled away, she waved and offered a brave smile. He returned the wave—a halfhearted flip of the hand—but not the smile.

The ride to her neighborhood took twenty-two minutes. Twenty-two minutes to wonder how much Ryan had loved his wife. Why they'd gotten divorced and if the miscarriage had anything to do with their going their separate ways.

Ah, well. Some things were never meant to be—her and Ryan. Better she found out now than to lose her heart to a man who'd never have her. How soon she'd forgotten the valuable lesson of moving from foster home to foster home: nothing lasted forever. Not even love.

"GRANDPA, it's me, Ryan." He shouldn't have phoned. But the train ride on the M subway line lasted forever and he needed a distraction. Conversation would keep his mind off a particular blonde who'd gotten under his skin.

"Good to hear from you, grandson. Happy birthday, by the way."

Now his grandfather would assume he'd called seeking a birthday greeting. He mumbled a heartfelt, "Thanks."

After years of rebuffing his family's efforts to reach out to him, he deserved to be snubbed. That his grandfather appreciated hearing from Ryan encouraged him to believe that when he got his head screwed on straight he'd be welcomed into the fold again.

"Spoke with your brother Nelson."

Ryan envied his elder brother. After meeting Nelson's fiancée, Ellen, he'd recognized immediately that the petite dairy farmer was a perfect partner for his headstrong, domineering brother. As the lone unattached brother, Ryan deemed himself an outsider. *You had your chance, but blew it.* "Have Nelson and Ellen set a wedding date?"

"They're getting married in Vegas sometime in January."

"Vegas?" Vegas wasn't Nelson's idea of fun.

"Ellen and Seth haven't traveled much and Nelson believes they'll enjoy the gaudiness of the Strip. I plan to bring my companion, Rosalie."

Companion? "You mean, Mrs. Padrõn?" Things must be getting serious between his grandfather and the woman Aaron had introduced him to this past spring.

"Enough about me and my girlfriend," his grandfather chortled. "What's going on?"

Leave it to the old man to sense that Ryan had another subject other than *hello* on his mind. "I could use some advice."

"You're speaking to the right man. I've got ninety-one years' worth of free counsel stored inside me."

Ryan chuckled. "A man I work with has a younger brother who's involved in a local gang. The kid's fifteen."

"Why is he hanging out with hoodlums?"

"Who understands why kids do anything. The teen wants out, but if he quits, the other gang members will hunt down him and his family."

"Sounds ominous for the boy, but I'm relieved to hear you're becoming involved with your coworkers."

"I wouldn't say I'm involved…." Ryan hedged. *Then why do you care about Willie and what happens to the boy?* Because Anna cared about the kid. And anything that hurt Joe's family would hurt Anna.

"Do you want me to intervene? I have a marker or two I can call in."

Markers? He didn't care to hear how his grandfather had acquired those. "It's none of my business, really." Besides, since 9/11 the old man and his brothers had been trying to rescue Ryan. *Then why did you call him if you didn't want his help?*

Because Anna's talk about the Smith family and roots had made Ryan recognize his loneliness. Made him long to travel back in time to before 9/11, when his relationship with his family hadn't been strained.

"Well, then, my boy, how are you?"

Ryan understood what his grandfather was really asking—was he surviving mingling with people on a daily basis. "I'm doing okay."

"Made any buddies on the job?"

Anna's face popped into Ryan's mind and he half smiled at his reflection in the window. "One." He considered Anna a *friend*. Telling her about Sandra's miscarriage had been difficult—although he hadn't confessed the entire truth.

"That's my boy. I've got to go now. I'm catching a late-night flight to L.A. Rosalie promised me breakfast in the morning."

"Are you serious about this Rosalie?"

"I might have to beg her to marry me. Wait until you try her chorizo sausage. The woman's an amazing cook." He chuckled. "She's a spring chicken at eighty-one, but she claims she's too old for me."

"I'm glad you're having fun together." Ryan meant it. His grandfather had been alone for over three decades. "You deserve to be happy."

"Take heart, grandson. You'll find happiness again."

"Take care, Grandpa."

Ryan snapped his cell phone shut and imagined the birthday cards waiting in the mailbox. The ones that each year landed in the trash unopened. He couldn't bear to read the heartfelt sentiments, the offers to listen if he needed to talk, offers to visit him. He closed his eyes and envisioned Anna's ready smile.

Tonight he'd find the courage to open the cards—because that was what Anna, his new friend, would instruct him to do.

Chapter Five

Ryan dribbled the basketball twice, faked a pass, then let it fly toward the hoop. *Swish!*

"We got ourselves a Kobe Bryant, guys," Antonio bellowed. He dribbled a ball to the three-point line and fired. The shot rocketed off the backboard, almost decapitating Joe.

"You can't shoot worth—" Joe glanced at the women and children in the bleachers "—spit."

"Give me a chance to warm up, will ya?" his teammate complained, then banged another ball off the rim.

Passing up an opportunity to shoot, Ryan handed the ball to Joe. At five feet eight inches the guy didn't have a prayer of snagging a rebound.

"Thanks, man," Joe mumbled.

Ryan wondered if he'd made a mistake in allowing Anna to talk him into playing in the YMCA Friday-night basketball game. She was nowhere in the stands and he feared she'd stay away because of him.

Earlier in the week a lunchtime argument over bad refereeing had evolved into "You ever shoot hoops, Jones?" Ryan hadn't talked basketball in ages and the topic had released a flood of memories—good memories. Memories of playing varsity ball all four years of high school. Of winning the district championship his senior year.

When Leon had announced yesterday that he couldn't make tonight's game, Anna had urged Ryan to fill in for the man. She'd argued that if he refused, the team would have to forfeit because the boss, Bobby, had gone to Atlantic City, leaving the team short one player. Ryan believed she wished for him to become more involved with the men, but the spirit of her encouragement had changed since their coffee date at the Muddy River.

Subtle changes. Changes he suspected only *he'd* noticed. Her smile had dimmed a few watts. She continued to pass out free hugs and pats on the back—save for Ryan. Anna didn't touch him. And when she glanced his way, her eyes skirted his face. He didn't want to believe that Anna was distancing herself from him when their friendship had barely gotten off the ground.

He never thought he'd admit it, but he'd gotten used to her crowding, prodding, pushy tendencies and found her aloofness unnerving. When she'd asked him to play with the team, he'd jumped at the chance to please her, hoping the basketball game would fix the problem that stood between them.

Another shot ricocheted off the backboard, snapping Ryan out of his reverie. He caught the ball and dribbled around Antonio, then launched a jumper from twenty feet. *Swoosh.*

"Show-off," Antonio grumbled, lifting his hand above his head for a high five.

Years had passed since Ryan had played any recreational basketball. He'd had reservations about his ability to shoot and was relieved he could launch the ball toward the basket after suffering extensive muscle damage to his left shoulder as a result of 9/11. He'd take the extra aches and pains tonight if the team walked away with a victory.

"We should demote Leon to water boy and make Ryan the starting guard for the rest of the season," Eryk suggested.

Before Ryan had the chance to tell the team he'd love to play in another game, the referee blew his whistle and called the team captains to the middle of the court.

"C'mon. Pam brought a cooler of drinks." Eryk trotted to the bench and Ryan followed.

"Aw, Pam. No sports drinks?" Eryk waved a juice bag with a cartoon character on the front.

"Sorry, honey. Didn't have time to stop by the store." Eryk's wife bolted from the bleachers and ran after a tyke heading for the exit.

"Here." Eryk flung the juice bag.

As Ryan fumbled with the straw attached to the side of the pouch, he decided he'd be better off using the water fountain. The scent of citrus drifted over his shoulder and he spun, then darn near swallowed his tongue. Wow. *Double wow*—Anna Nowakowski in a cheerleading outfit.

"That's one way to open the drink." She nodded to the bag he had a death grip on. "Squeeze until it bursts."

To heck with his thirst. He dropped the juice into the cooler and gave his full attention to Anna's outfit. "You have great legs." He cringed. Did *friends* say those things to each other?

Cheeks pink, she murmured, "Thanks."

Her long blond hair had been secured with red-and-white ribbons, which matched her red-and-white pleated skirt, the short-sleeved sweater and even the red ruffles around her bobby socks. "Watch out for those guys." She nodded to the team shooting at the other end of the court. "The Bulls are nasty."

Except for their jerseys, the opposing players didn't appear threatening. Don's Electrical was stamped across the material, and underneath a stick figure with its hair standing on end held a live wire.

Fifteen minutes later Ryan discovered how dirty Don's Electrical played. When Ryan drove the lane for a layup, his opponent hammered him and he ended up flat on his back gasping for air. Served him right for daydreaming about how hot Anna looked in her outfit, instead of focusing on the game. The blurry outline of Joe's hand wavered in front of Ryan's face and he accepted help off the floor.

The upright position allowed oxygen to flow freely to his lungs, and in seconds his vision cleared. Something compelled him to check the bleachers and he spotted Anna with her hands clasped over her mouth and a deer-in-the-headlights expression on her face. Her concern went a long way in easing the throbbing pain in his elbow, which had hit the floor first when he'd gotten his legs knocked out from under him. He flashed a strained smile, but it wasn't until he'd made both free throws that she took her seat on the bench again.

There was no time to analyze Anna's reaction, because the same terminator who'd decked him now dribbled circles around Antonio. Ryan left his player to help out and managed to steal the ball, then lob it across court to Patrick, who stood in the lane, hands on his knees breathing hard. Everyone in the stands yelled,

"Pat, heads up!" Startled, the man caught the ball a second before it would have bounced off his head. He dribbled in for a layup and brought the team to within ten points of the Bulls.

The buzzer trilled and the players retreated to their respective benches for a time-out before the final two minutes of the game. Ryan jogged toward the water fountain at the end of the gym but stopped when Anna called his name. She climbed over two girls scribbling in coloring books to hand him a sports drink.

"Thanks." Ryan guzzled half the bottle, then came up for air. "You were right. This team is rough."

"We can win if *you* shoot the ball," she whispered.

"Me?"

"Be a ball hog."

"You've played the game before, haven't you?"

"One of my foster brothers taught me. You met him the other night at the Muddy River."

The guy he'd been jealous of had been her foster brother?

"I'd planned to pass the ball inside to Antonio and let him get fouled." Ryan had no desire to end up on the floor again.

"Antonio's a horrible free-throw shooter. You're better off jacking up three-pointers."

Having never argued basketball with a woman before, Ryan found Anna's intensity amusing. "The team won't invite me to play again if I don't share."

"They will if you win the game," she promised, inching closer, the front of her sweater brushing his arm.

Maybe he'd imagined her remoteness this past week. "I could use a little motivation."

One side of her mouth curved. "Would a victory kiss from me suffice?"

Her answer knocked out what little breath remained in his lungs after four quarters of full-court basketball. Glad the old Anna had returned, he lowered his voice. "Deal." He'd forgotten how fun flirting with a woman could be and grinned like a buffoon. He wasn't as confident in his ability to pull off the win as Anna was, but he'd give it one hell of a try. "Prepare to pucker, my lady."

The referee blew his whistle, signaling the end of the time-out. In the team huddle, Ryan announced, "I'm going to hog the ball and shoot three-pointers."

"Anna tell you to do that?" Joe asked.

"Yep."

"Whatever Anna says goes," Patrick declared. Antonio and Eryk agreed and went to inbound the ball.

Offered the green light, Ryan tore up the court. His three-pointers hit nothing but net. With fifteen seconds left in the game, Parnell Brothers trailed by one point and Don's Electrical had possession of the ball.

All heck broke loose. Ryan knocked the ball from the hands of the opponent. Eryk scrambled after the loose ball and managed to throw it inbounds before stepping over the end line. Ryan caught it and dribbled. "Shoot! Shoot the ball!" greeted his ears as he crossed center court. With two seconds remaining on the clock, he launched a prayer.

An eerie silence settled over the gym and right as the buzzer sounded… *Swish!* The bleachers erupted into chaos. Women screamed, and kids ran onto the court to hug their fathers. Ryan chuckled as Antonio struggled to keep his shorts from falling to his ankles when his son shimmied up his legs.

Joy. Pure, sweet joy filled Ryan as he absorbed the pandemonium. He couldn't remember the last time his actions had resulted in such excitement. The men kissed their wives and girlfriends, hugged their children and rooster-strutted around the floor. Ryan got clobbered over the head with a pom-pom before Anna flung her arms around his neck. Automatically, he wrapped her in his embrace and twirled. Her laughter warmed his heart.

The squishy softness of Anna's well-endowed bosom pressing into his chest brought forth an image in Ryan's head of the two of them tangled in bedsheets. After another twirl it occurred to him that *he* smelled a little *too* healthy to be this close to her. He loosened his hold, but she stuck to him. If he didn't know better, he'd believe she intended for everyone to assume they were a couple.

Would that be a bad thing? Maybe. Maybe not. He'd been a loner for so many years he couldn't remember how to be a *couple.* Besides, hadn't he decided friendship was the best road to travel with Anna?

"Told you I was right." Her eyes twinkled.

"Hey, hotshot," Antonio called as he untangled his son from his legs, then held him up in the air by the scruff of his collar. "We're heading over to Mimi's."

"Dinner and drinks are on us, Kobe," Joe teased.

Not be left out, Eryk chimed in, "That's right. The MVP doesn't pay for his meal."

Playing basketball with the guys was one thing, but he wasn't ready to dine with their families. "They wouldn't have invited you, Ryan, if they didn't want you to celebrate with them." Anna's assurance chipped away at his resolve to keep to himself.

"Sounds good," he hollered to the group.

Right in front of everyone, the guys whipped off their

sweaty jerseys and threw on clean T-shirts. Anna gazed expectantly at him, her attention shifting from his face to his chest. *Not going to happen.* He wasn't sharing his scars with anyone, especially not his *friend,* Anna.

When the men had finished toweling off their sweaty faces and damp hair, they collected their families and left the gym. Ryan grabbed the sports bag he'd stowed under the bleachers. "I'll be right out," he promised, then disappeared through the doorway marked Men's Locker Room.

Inside, he shoved his head under the sink and rinsed his hair and face. Then he used a wad of damp paper towels to wipe the sweat from the rest of his torso. A liberal dousing of deodorant, a clean shirt and pair of jeans and he was good to go.

"Sorry about the delay," he apologized when he noticed Anna holding up the wall outside the locker room.

She sniffed. "You smell good."

He raised an eyebrow. "I believe you have a debt to pay."

"Don't worry." Her eyes twinkled. "Before the night is out, you'll get your victory kiss."

BY THE TIME Anna and Ryan arrived at Mimi's Pizzeria on Forest Avenue, she wondered what had happened to Ryan's good mood. The tight lines around his mouth convinced her that he'd rather haul heavy construction debris to a Dumpster than join the team for a celebration dinner. His fault—he should have missed more shots.

Anna had urged him to join the team celebration tonight in part because she'd regretted the way she'd acted this past week and wanted to make amends. The news of his ex-wife's miscarriage had devastated her.

She'd needed time to accept that her developing feelings for Ryan had nowhere to go. Keeping her distance had been a self-preservation tactic. But she'd been miserable and her misery had been compounded by the puppy-dog confusion on Ryan's face each time she'd avoided him.

After a heart-to-heart talk with her roommate, she'd realized that she and Ryan were a long way from a serious relationship. For goodness' sake, they hadn't even kissed—an activity she planned to remedy tonight. As long as her relationship with Ryan didn't stray from the flirty-and-fun path, she saw no harm in the two of them becoming better acquainted. Tonight, her goal was to help Ryan relax and enjoy himself.

"Crowded," he commented, holding open the restaurant door.

"You won't be disappointed. Mimi's has the best pizza in Queens. I eat here a lot because it's close to my apartment."

As soon as they entered, Eryk hollered, "Hey, the hero of the game!" He waved them over to a cluster of tables shoved together in the far corner.

When Ryan hesitated, Anna casually slipped her hand into his and led them toward the group. Mismatched tables and chairs sat on a painted concrete floor in the boisterous hole-in-the-wall eatery. Poster-size black-and-white historical photographs of Queens decorated the whitewashed brick walls. The heavy aroma of oregano and garlic floated through the air.

Before they reached the tables, a miniature Tasmanian devil spun out of nowhere, knocking into Ryan's knees before twirling off in a new direction. "Mark, walk," Anna warned Antonio's youngest son. The little imp smiled and dashed away.

"Have a seat, Kobe." Joe pulled out a chair for Ryan.

The women and girlfriends had congregated at one end of the long table and the men at the other. With a last reassuring squeeze, Anna released Ryan's hand and joined the ladies.

"So..." Eryk's wife, Pam, grinned. As a matter of fact, all the women wore silly grins.

Playing dumb, Anna asked, "So, what?"

Patrick's girlfriend, Dolly, nodded toward the other end of the table. "S-o...*him.*"

Anna was fond of Dolly, a no-nonsense vet tech who ran a pet-boarding business on the side. And she admired how Dolly raved over Patrick's choir voice to anyone who would listen. Hoping to steer the topic in a different direction, she asked, "Has Patrick recovered from Father Baynard's tongue-lashing?"

A blush spread across the younger woman's cheeks. "Pat's terrified my uncle's going to demand we wed." Dolly giggled. "My father knocked up my mother when she was sixteen, so Uncle Baynard fears I'm going to follow in her footsteps."

"But you're twenty-six," Antonio's wife, Lisa, noted.

"Exactly." Dolly rolled her eyeballs toward the other end of the table. "Forget Father Baynard. What about you and Ryan?"

Saved from answering by the sudden appearance of the waitress, Anna ordered a tap beer. Antonio slapped Ryan on the shoulder and announced, "He's drinking Bud with the rest of us."

A strained smile teased the corners of Ryan's mouth.

Call it a hunch, but Anna suspected Ryan would have preferred an uptown Heineken over a working-man's Budweiser.

While the men rehashed the game, Anna asked Joe's girlfriend, Linda, "Any leads on a teaching job?" Linda had recently completed her early-childhood-education degree and was in the process of obtaining her teacher certification and applying for jobs in various school districts.

"Next week I have an interview with an elementary school on Long Island. Keep your fingers crossed. If I get the job, I plan to drag Joe to the altar."

"Good luck. I had to have two of Antonio's babies before he found the courage to marry me." Lisa smiled lovingly at her husband. "He was terrified of fatherhood."

Lisa had shared with Anna that Antonio's father had beaten him as a young boy and Antonio had been worried he'd repeat the sins of his father with his own children. The exact opposite had happened. Antonio was nothing but a softie where the kids were concerned and Lisa complained that she had to be the disciplinarian.

Casting a surreptitious glance in Ryan's direction, Anna contemplated what kind of father he would have made if his baby had survived. Better than the mother she'd been—he'd have never given up his child. She imagined a dark-eyed little boy with blond hair... *Not in this lifetime, Anna.*

"Eryk confessed that the guy doesn't talk about himself," Pam interjected, ending Anna's daydream.

"Leon said Ryan mentioned he was divorced." Anna wondered who had been more at fault in Ryan's failed marriage, he or his wife. Had the miscarriage been the final straw in an already bad relationship?

"Ask him on a date," Linda encouraged.

"He's not my type." No sense allowing the girls to get their hopes up that she and Ryan might become a couple. Besides, however far they decided to take their relationship was nobody's business but theirs.

Pam finished her beer, caught her husband's attention and raised the glass in the air. Eryk nodded, then waved over the waitress.

"You have him well trained." Anna raised her beer mug in a toast.

"As long as I let Eryk *think* he's the boss, and scratch his itch once in a while, he obeys like a well-heeled dog." After the waitress delivered Pam's beer, she puckered her lips and made a loud kissing sound in her husband's direction. Poor Eryk blushed.

"What a flirt," Anna accused her.

"Speaking of flirting, have you and—"

"Mama," Lisa's son, Mark, interrupted Pam. The little boy tugged on his mother's pant leg and whined, "More money."

"Okay, sweetie." From her purse Lisa extracted a plastic sandwich bag of quarters. She stuffed the boy's jean pockets until they bulged. "That should hold you for a while and prevent you from tearing up the place." The five-year-old waddled to his father and raised his arms for a hug.

Anna caught the wistful expression on Ryan's face as he witnessed Antonio and Mark hug. Maybe Ryan's initial reluctance to join the group tonight had more to do with being around their children than around her or the adults. She considered making up an excuse to leave and escaping with Ryan, but just then the pizzas arrived. Mark dashed off to round up the other kids in the arcade room and a minute later little people crowded around the table. Mimicking chipmunks, they gobbled their pizza, then raced away, cheeks bulging with food.

While the adults dug into the remaining slices, Anna noticed Mark had reappeared at Ryan's side. The child's gaze shifted between Ryan's face and the piece of sausage on his plate. Ryan glanced at Antonio, but the dad was involved in a heated dispute with Patrick. After a moment, Ryan stabbed the meat with his fork and popped it into the boy's mouth. Mark chewed, then crawled into Ryan's lap and rested his head on his chest.

When Anna glanced at Ryan's face, her heart sank. Wearing a frozen mask of pain, he had his hands hovering above Mark's back, as if touching the child would cause immense pain. After a minute Mark scrambled off Ryan's lap and scurried away. Ryan's tormented eyes connected with hers. She dug out a twenty from her purse and tossed it on the table. "I need to get going," she announced, then stood. Ryan placed his napkin on the table, relief softening the lines around his mouth.

"Eryk and I can give you a lift." Pam frowned at Anna's abrupt announcement.

"Thanks, but Ryan will walk me home." Anna ignored Dolly's raised eyebrows and Lisa's mischievous smirk. "Good game, guys. See you Monday." Anna wove through the tables to the exit. Ryan joined her outside.

"Everything all right?" she asked.

His gaze fastened to a crack running through the sidewalk. "Couldn't be better."

Biting her tongue, she remained silent and waited for him to explain. His attention remained on the cement. "My apartment is a few blocks from here," she said.

"Fine."

The dull note in his voice didn't escape Anna. With sinking spirits, she mumbled, "You're tired. You should go home and rest." She stepped around him, but he snagged her sweater sleeve.

"I'll see you home." His expression dared her to argue.

They had strolled in silence for three blocks when Anna decided to throw caution to the wind. She nodded at a building across the street. "That was my first foster home."

"A bakery?"

"It wasn't a bakery when I lived in the second-floor apartment."

He threaded his fingers through hers. "How old were you?"

"Four." They continued walking and Anna basked in the warm comfort of Ryan's grasp. "The first year I lived with Mrs. Lowenstein was rough, but I adjusted. After a while, transferring from home to home—" she shrugged "—became a normal way of life."

They'd eaten up another block when she asked, "Do the guys expect you to play for them every week?"

"They said I could if I wanted."

He didn't sound too excited. "Are you going to?" More basketball games meant more pizza, more walks home, more time with Ryan.

"I might."

Better than a *no*. "I noticed Mark made a pest of himself around you tonight."

"Mark?"

"Lisa and Antonio's little boy."

A fleeting smile—painful in its brevity. "He's a cute kid."

"I have a question." Anna held her breath. Ryan wouldn't be the first person to request she mind her own business. She had a habit of poking her big Polish nose in people's affairs—with good intentions, of course. But not everyone appreciated the fine art of meddling.

"Shoot." He dropped her hand and shoved his fingers into his jean pockets.

"You said your ex-wife had a miscarriage. Do you have other children?"

They stopped at the iron gate in front of her brownstone apartment. "Nice place," he complimented, as if he'd never heard her question.

"Thanks." Anna was proud of the row house built by Germans in the twentieth century. The warm brown-brick facade sported an elegant bow front and crisp white trim. An extra-wide sidewalk, no garages, no off-street parking and a no-garbage-cans-out-front rule made her block a tiny utopia in a densely populated area.

He shifted his focus from her front door to her face. "No, there aren't any other children. Although I'd always hoped to be a father."

"I'm sorry things didn't work out with your wife." The sentiment sounded hollow. No matter how she tried, she couldn't smother the tiny flicker of gladness that Ryan's marriage had failed. Otherwise, she'd never have met him. She'd known him a short while, but already he'd snuck past her defenses.

"Someone's watching us," he muttered.

A silhouette hovered behind the curtain across the front window. "Blair's a regular watchdog." She fumbled with the gate latch and Ryan's hand covered hers.

"Aren't you forgetting…?" he reminded her in a hoarse whisper.

Chapter Six

No way was Ryan walking off without collecting his victory kiss from Anna. Her promise was the one thing that had kept him from bolting out of Mimi's Pizzeria. The entire evening had been an emotional roller-coaster ride. He wanted to forget everything but Anna and him. And the kiss she'd promised.

The tiny flecks of amethyst in her shimmering blue eyes—wide, innocent eyes—pledged a haven for battered hearts and bruised souls. The temptation to hand himself over to her for safekeeping jarred Ryan.

They hardly knew each other, yet he'd connected with Anna on a level he'd never experienced with any other person—even his ex-wife. Without speaking a word, he sensed Anna understood his thoughts and feelings—as if their souls had met in a prior life light-years away from the here and now.

Anna the enigma. On the outside happy and cheerful. On the inside—heartbreakingly lonely. What was her secret from the world?

Does it matter? It's just a kiss.

Because she was special, he refused to hurt her.

Refused to believe there was more between them than—
Shut up and kiss her.

His gaze dropped to her mouth and he savored the hot rush of anticipation that seized his loins. Her tongue licked her lower lip, leaving a glistening trail across the plump flesh. Then she purred—a barely audible sigh of need.

Full and *soft* and *giving* were the words that came to mind when he settled his mouth over hers. One touch and he yearned for more than her mouth. He wanted all of her. Against him. In him. Around him. Tangling his fingers in her long hair, he titled her head. *Perfect.* He thrust his tongue inside and tasted.

Sweet. So sweet. He couldn't get enough.

The kiss spiraled into a desperate urgency. If not for the full moon spotlighting them, Ryan would have been tempted to collect more than a kiss from Anna. He had a hunch she would do nothing to stop him. That hunch might as well have been a cold bucket of water over his head.

He broke off the kiss and tucked her head against his shoulder. He didn't dare glance into her eyes— pools of blue quicksand capable of sucking him under. Anna's lips nudged his throat, and he shivered from the sensation.

"Cold?" She clasped his forearms, then slowly slid her fingers up his flesh, edging under his T-shirt sleeve.

"Wow." His fingers dug into her shoulders as he forced space between them. He gentled his grip when she winced, and cursed himself for allowing the moment to get out of hand. Shoot, he'd wanted *out of hand* until her fingers had grazed his puckered flesh. "You're an excellent promise keeper, Ms. Nowakowski." He brushed a strand of hair from her cheek—any excuse to touch her.

"Hmm." She tapped a long fingernail against her

chin, her eyes sparkling with humor. "Shall we negotiate another promise for next week's game?"

"Do I have to sink the winning shot for the team?"

"Of course." Anna's soft breath caressed his cheek.

Oh, man. Could he keep it together for a second kiss?
"Are you always this sassy?"

"It's the outfit." Her mouth inched closer…closer…

Saved by the porch light!

"Darn." Anna scowled at the shadow still present in
the window. "Would you care to come inside?"

Yes, his mind shouted; he was convinced his loneliness
would find solace within the walls of Anna's home. But
at what price? He'd lost his soul to 9/11. He couldn't afford
to give away the one thing keeping him alive—his heart.

Big blue eyes begged him to risk everything and
follow her beyond the gate. He yearned to see her apartment—the color of the walls, the furniture, the decora-
tions, even the food in the refrigerator. But not tonight.
Maybe not ever. She deserved better than a man whose
scars cut deep below the skin's surface. "I'm sorry," he
muttered, then did an about-face and walked away,
hoping…fearing she'd call out to him.

Nothing. Cold, bitter silence escorted him to the
corner. At the intersection, he paused, resisting the
temptation to glance over his shoulder. Was she rooted
to the sidewalk, watching? The light changed. He cut
across the street and veered right toward the M subway
line, which would transport him back to his apartment—
no longer the refuge it had once been.

As the bright headlight of the train drew near, Ryan
wondered if Anna would agree to an affair. Light, flir-
tatious, fun—an Anna-type fling. The whistle sounded,
the blast clearing the stupid idea out of his head. What

made him believe he'd find the courage to climb naked into bed with a woman? Besides, Anna deserved better than a fling. Better than a man with one-sided intentions—his side.

"JONES, GET IN HERE," Bobby Parnell hollered from the hallway outside his office.

"Boss sounds ticked," Joe teased. "What happened?"

"Heck if I know." Ryan hadn't spoken to Parnell since Monday—four days ago—when the boss had congratulated him on winning the basketball game.

"If he fires you, can I have the rest of your sandwich?" Eryk grinned.

Ryan shoved the remainder of his lunch across the table, then left the break room.

"Shut the door," Parnell instructed after Ryan entered the office. "Sit."

A dog command. Ryan clenched his jaw to keep from objecting and reclined in the chair facing the boss's cluttered desk—an almost-empty jumbo-size bottle of antacid tablets, diet-cola cans, sticky notes hanging off the edges and three different newspapers opened to the sports page spread across the top.

"Normally, I don't poke my nose into my employees' private affairs." A smile tugged at the corners of his mouth. "Anna usually takes care of that." The smile vanished. "Since this concerns Anna…" Parnell paused, as if he expected Ryan to fill in the blank. "Mind if I ask what's going on between you two?"

Yeah, I do mind. "Nothing." That is, if Ryan had his way. After mulling over the idea of a fling with Anna, he'd decided it was in their—okay, his—best interest to forget the kiss they'd shared. He'd intended to talk to her on Monday, but when he'd arrived at the station, he'd learned Anna would be out of the office most of the week, attending a software seminar for a new computer program the company planned to implement. She was expected to return later this afternoon.

"Then the kiss you two shared last Friday meant nothing?"

Ryan hadn't figured Anna a kiss-and-tell gal. "How did you hear about that?"

"Anna's very highly thought of in her neighborhood, Jones. She does a lot of nice things for people, and in return folks keep an eye on her."

"Did her roommate tattle on us?" Ryan asked.

"Nope. Three neighbors."

Three well-meaning Peeping Toms had witnessed their kiss?

"They'd appreciate you stating your intentions toward Anna."

"My intentions aren't anybody's business but my own," Ryan protested. He'd never answered to anyone, not even his grandfather—at least, about women.

"You'd better treat her with respect." Parnell squinted. "If you don't, you'll deal with me. Understand?"

"The neighborhood watch has nothing to worry about. Kissing Anna was a mistake I don't intend to repeat." He popped out of the chair, faced the door, then froze.

Pale blue eyes round as saucers blinked from the doorway. Anna's shattered expression sliced through Ryan. How long had she been standing there?

"If you two need to talk…" Parnell made a move to leave but Anna held up a hand.

"I believe Ryan had the last word." She spun on her sensible low-heeled shoes and retreated from the office.

Parnell's words stopped Ryan at the door. "You'd better make things right between you and Anna, Jones."

With a nod of understanding, he left, his mind searching for a way to erase the hurt from Anna's eyes. But how? He found her on the front stoop, arms hugging her middle as she stared into space.

"Anna, I'm—"

"Don't," she warned, facing him. The hurt had faded from her eyes, replaced by the steely glint of a well-seasoned warrior. Stoic. Dangerous. He suspected years in foster care had contributed to the self-protective instinct. Too bad the same skills hadn't been ingrained in him from childhood. Maybe then he'd have escaped his divorce intact instead of in pieces.

The door creaked open and Patrick announced, "We're heading out in five minutes."

"I'll catch up." Ryan moved toward Anna but stopped when she backed up to the edge of the step. He didn't want to risk her tumbling to the sidewalk. "Let me explain."

"What's to explain? You regret kissing me." She made an attempt to move past him but he blocked her.

"I don't regret our kiss." He had to find the words to make her understand.

"But you don't intend to kiss me again?" she challenged.

Frustrated, he shoved a hand through his hair. "I'm not ready to get serious with you. With anyone." Serious meant intimate. Intimate meant emotionally messy. He didn't want any messes. "It's best if we forget about the kiss."

Was he crazy? "I can't," Anna argued. Why did she have to be attracted to such an obstinate, confusing man? *Good grief.* She'd honestly believed they'd ex-changed more than slobber during their kiss. "We're both adults, Ryan. I noticed—" she quirked an eyebrow "—your attraction to me."

"I'm not denying I'm attracted to you," he admitted. "But my job here is temporary. I'll be gone in seven weeks."

A corner of Anna's heart tore. Seven weeks was a lifetime to a woman who'd already waited forever for a man as special as Ryan to happen along. "Do you have to leave?" She'd cold-call companies and bring in extra business. Bobby would be forced to keep Ryan on.

"I think it's best if I do."

"You're acting as though I'm pushing for marriage." She'd dreamed it. The night he'd kissed her after the basketball game, she'd curled up on the couch and had confessed to her roommate how Ryan had made her feel twittery inside. To herself she'd admitted she fantasized about marrying him. But fantasies were fantasies and real life was real life. After learning of his ex-wife's mis-carriage, Anna was certain his last few weeks on the job would be the only *forever* she'd have with him. "I thought we were friends."

The confusion in his eyes lent her hope. "What kind of friends?" he asked.

"Coffee. Movie. Dinner." Maybe more. Hopefully more.

"Friends don't kiss, right?" He was caving in.

The garage door rose, saving her from answering.

"Give me some time to think about it." He hustled to the garage.

At least he hadn't said no. A moment later, the dump truck pulled away from the station. Her heart thumped when her eyes connected with Ryan's through the windshield. His hangdog expression hinted that time was the last thing he desired from her.

MAYBE SHE DIDN'T show up at the game because she does errands on Saturdays.

She didn't show because yesterday you complained you needed time.

Tired of listening to the dueling voices in his head, Ryan parked his Lexus around the corner from Anna's apartment and shut off the engine.

The end of the first week in October had arrived. Cloudy and blustery—a typical fall day for New York City. Wind gusts mugged people dashing in and out of stores, whipping hair in faces and threatening to steal shopping bags. The gloomy weather matched his mood.

Guilt. Ryan couldn't recall the last time he'd suffered a bout of good old-fashioned remorse. He'd arrived at the YMCA gym this morning for the basketball game, anticipating Anna in her sexy cheerleading outfit. She'd been conspicuously absent.

When she hadn't made an appearance by halftime, the wives and girlfriends had pounced. They'd asked him Anna's whereabouts—as if their one kiss had qualified them for couple status. Although he'd claimed ignorance regarding Anna's location, their feminine glares had burned holes in his jersey the entire game—which they'd lost.

He'd asked Anna for time. Not space. He'd never intended to keep her from her friends. After the game, he'd declined an invitation to join the team for lunch. Instead, he planned to pay Anna a visit and put an end to the strain between them. He'd convinced himself that nothing existed between them but a kiss and a fair amount of sexual attraction.

When he'd begun working at Parnell Brothers she'd driven him nuts with her meddling, caring ways. But after a few weeks he'd grown accustomed to the smothering. In fact, he anticipated the extra attention she showered on him. This morning, when she hadn't shown up at the game, he'd been forced to admit he missed her.

Friends... How could he be *just friends* with Anastazia Nowakowski when he genuinely cared for her and was sexually attracted to her? Combine *care* with *sexual attraction* and the direction the relationship was headed was straight to *bed*—the one place he dared not go with her.

No way would he allow another woman to tear him up the way his ex-wife had. He didn't believe Anna capable of intentionally hurting him, but he couldn't, wouldn't, put his heart on the line a second time. Which left them one option: *friends.*

With that thought in mind, he exited the car and set the alarm. When he came around the corner, he glanced ahead to her brownstone. He'd taken three steps when the apartment door opened. And a *man* stepped out?

Caught by surprise, Ryan froze, his feet cemented to the sidewalk. He blinked. Once. Twice. The guy wasn't a mirage. Dressed in black slacks and a white dress shirt, he struggled with his tie. Anna followed him outside and tied the knot. Smiling, she brushed her hands over his shoulders as if dusting fine hairs or lint off the shirt. The jerk kissed her cheek. Anna called after him and the guy waved a hand over his head as he cut across the street and disappeared around the corner.

By the time Ryan returned his attention to the brownstone, Anna had disappeared inside. He rubbed his chest, wondering at the stiff sensation beneath his ribs. The tightness hardened into a burning lump. He'd been empty inside for so long that the burst of jealousy caught him off guard. When Anna retreated, she went all the way—to another man!

What a fool to believe *he* was the reason she'd stayed away from the basketball game this morning. How had he allowed Anna to slip beneath his defenses?

Friends, remember?

He hurried to the apartment, taking the steps two at a time. Then he rang the bell, pressing his finger against the black button longer than necessary. The door swung open.

Anna… She wore a faded New York Giants football jersey three sizes too big and a pair of ratty jeans with holes in the knees. Pink socks peeked out from under the frayed hem of the denim. Her hair was in a messy pile on her head and held in place with a clip. She wore no makeup, lip gloss or dangling earrings, so that her big nose jumped off her face.

She'd never looked more beautiful.

Forcing his gaze from her face, he demanded, "Who was that?"

"Who's who?" She poked her head around his shoulder and glanced up the block.

"The guy whose tie you fixed."

"You mean Blair?"

The name sounded familiar, but Ryan couldn't remember where he'd heard it before. "Is he your lover or just a *friend?*"

Her full lips curved upward, lighting her blue eyes. "Blair is my roommate."

"Roommate?" Now he recalled where he'd hear that

name—from the other guys at work. But he'd assumed Blair was a girl's name.

"Blair and I have shared this apartment for three years."

Three years and just roommates. Right. They must have crossed the line at one time or another. "So, you're not involved with him?"

Her sunny smile slid off her face. "No. Not that it's any of your business, *friend.*"

Ouch. "Have you slept with him in the past?" he persisted.

"Not in the past and not in the future." One eyebrow arched. "Blair prefers men."

Ryan struggled to digest the news that Anna's roommate was gay. He wanted to believe her, but he'd seen the guy with his own eyes. Surfer-style blond hair, tall and broad shouldered—a male model or aspiring actor. The opposite of *him.* "You're positive he's…"

"Yes." She planted her hands on her hips. "Didn't the team have a basketball game today?"

"We lost."

"That's too bad. Now, if you don't mind…" She reached for the doorknob, but he snagged her hand.

"Wait." What could he say to prevent her from shutting him out? Right then his stomach rumbled. "I'm hungry," he blurted. "Let me take you to lunch."

"No, thanks. I'm having Blair's homemade chicken-noodle soup." Leaving the door ajar, she called over her shoulder, "You're welcome to stay."

An olive branch. At the very least, he owed her an apology for his Neanderthal behavior. He stepped inside, then secured the door. The first word that came to mind was *color.* Everywhere. Unlike his shades-of-gray living quarters, reds and golds warmed the walls, and dark oak trim and flooring added richness to the living space. A fabric-covered sofa sat by the window. Two overstuffed matching chairs in a lime-and-cream stripe faced a coffee table covered with cooking magazines. The table rested on an Oriental rug in the middle of the room.

Black-and-white studio portraits in ornate gold-flecked frames arranged artfully along the walls drew his attention next. He moved across the room to study them. Since Anna had grown up in foster homes, he assumed the pictures belonged to her roommate.

"I bought them at estate sales," Anna observed from the kitchen doorway.

"They aren't long-lost relatives, are they?"

She shook her head.

Intrigued, he asked, "Why did you buy them?"

"Because I don't have a family of my own and I wanted one."

Her candor startled Ryan.

"That's Marcus you're looking at." Anna shuffled into the room.

"You named these people?"

She motioned to the portrait. "I always imagined having a father who favored this man."

The dark-haired, middle-aged gentleman wore an ascot and possessed kind eyes and a hint of a mischievous smile. "Marcus" had a good heart and a sense of humor. He was the kind of man who would never abandon his child, as Anna's biological father had abandoned her.

"How many pretend family members do you have?"

"Twenty-three," she boasted, indicating more framed photos along the dining-room wall.

Ryan studied the faces watching him from the walls.

Why would Anna surround herself with pretend relatives when she could have easily married and started a family of her own by now?

Unless…Anna, too, was hiding from the world—but out in the open, instead of behind closed doors like Ryan.

Chapter Seven

"I'll purchase Boardwalk for four hundred," Ryan announced after he rolled a six and moved the top hat to the Monopoly property next to GO.

"And you said you weren't any good at board games," Anna grumped, accepting the five-hundred-dollar bill Ryan handed her. She issued him a hundred in change from the bank, all the while resisting the urge not to squirm under his penetrating stare. They'd been playing the game for over an hour, and several times she'd glanced up to discover Ryan studying her. So far she'd resisted the urge to run over to the mirror and check for bits of noodles or chicken stuck in her teeth from lunch.

She rolled the dice and moved three spaces. "Blair offered to buy me the newest version of Monopoly, which uses Visa and debit cards instead of paper money, but I'm rather fond of the blue, pink and yellow bills."

Flashing a smug grin, Ryan handed her more cash. "Add these pretty bills to the bank. I'm buying a hotel for Marvin Gardens."

"Greedy man." She slid the hotel across the board and motioned to the red hotels covering Illinois, Indiana and Kentucky Avenues. "With my luck, I'll be in debt to you for a hundred thousand dollars before I travel one more time around the board."

"Once I have you backed into the corner, I can afford to be generous." His words teased, but his eyes flashed with double meaning.

Caught off balance—a condition suffered frequently around Ryan—she rolled the dice, then moved her thimble five spaces to Community Chest. She plucked the yellow card off the top of the pile. "'Pay school tax of $150.'"

Rich, baritone laughter filled the dining room, the sound resonating deep within Anna…warming her. "You should do that more often," she insisted.

"Do what?"

"Laugh."

An emotionless mask slid over his face, and his gaze latched onto the game piece he fiddled with.

Why hadn't she kept the comment to herself? The way Ryan blew off his teammate's praise during the basketball game a week ago should have warned her that he preferred not to draw attention to himself. Although she appreciated that he wasn't a man who thrived on others' admiration, she reasoned Ryan carried his humbleness too far by avoiding people altogether.

After he'd finished two helpings of Blair's homemade soup, she'd waited for him to make a dash for the door. Instead, he'd surprised her with an announcement that he intended to visit awhile. They'd sat on the couch in the living room and chatted about inconsequential things, while drizzle wet the pavement. When the subject shifted to favorite hobbies on rainy days, Anna had challenged Ryan to a game of Monopoly. To her surprise, he'd accepted, offering hope that he wished to give *friendship* an honest try.

For the past hour she'd gone crazy with wanting—to kiss him. She hadn't been able to forget the taste of his mouth or the feel of his lips against hers. Even though she'd convinced herself that a serious relationship with Ryan was out of the question, her body hadn't received the message.

"Here's my school-tax money." She waved the paper bills in the air, but Ryan's attention rested on the portrait hanging above the hutch. Taken in the early 1920s, it showed an elderly woman wearing a cloche—a close-fitting hat—which complimented her sleek, gray bobbed hairdo. Obviously, the lady had caught his interest.

In truth, after Anna had revealed her pretend family to Ryan, she'd expected him to assume she was a kook—at the very least, insane. But again he'd surprised her. Instead of mockery, sympathy had shone in his steady brown gaze—as if he understood her pain, her loneliness, her need to feel connected to someone and not be alone in the world. "That's Viola. She was sassy, outspoken, educated and loved to dance the Charleston."

"And how are you related?" he played along.

"My grandmother."

A sad smile tipped the corners of his mouth. "My parents and grandmother died in a plane crash when I was two years old." Ryan hadn't spilled his guts, but coming from such a private man the statement was a treasure trove of information.

"I'm sorry." A hot lump clogged Anna's throat. They'd both lost their parents at an early age. "Who raised you?"

"My grandfather." The note of affection in his voice testified to a childhood filled with love despite the loss of a mother and father. How fortunate for him.

"Did your grandfather ever remarry?"

"Nope." Ryan's face softened as he spoke of his grandfather. "All those years he'd insisted he didn't have time for women or marriage. He claimed my grandmother had been the love of his life and he didn't have room in his heart for another woman."

Did Ryan feel the same way about his ex-wife? Had the woman once been the love of his life?

"We went through several nannies over the years," Ryan continued. "But each evening, our grandfather tucked us three boys in bed."

Anna clasped Ryan's hand, her fingers threading through his, turning her insides mushy when he stroked his thumb across the center of her palm. "If you don't mind my asking, why weren't you and your brothers on the plane with your parents and grandmother?"

"They'd planned an adult vacation. My brothers and I had been left in the care of a nanny for the weekend. Grandpa was to meet up with them at the ski resort. Thank God he had a business meeting that had delayed him, or my brothers and I would have been orphaned." He winced. "I'm sorry, Anna. That was thoughtless."

"Don't worry." She waved off his concern. "I cried all my tears years ago." At least, she hoped so. Sometimes she wondered at her bouts of melancholy. "The guys at work and their families have adopted me. We look after one another."

"And Charlie," Ryan added.

"Yeah, Charlie's a good guy. We lived a year with the

Clemsons and became as close as any biological brother and sister. Even though he graduated from high school three years ahead of me, he's stayed in the area and keeps in touch." Before Ryan had a chance to fire off another question, she asked, "What about you? I assume your grandfather has passed away. Are you and your siblings close?"

Ryan chuckled. "At ninety-one, Grandpa's alive and kicking."

"Amazing." She motioned to the wall in the living room. "He's outlived half of my portrait family."

Stretching his arms over his head, Ryan yawned—the movement meant to appear casual, but Anna understood better. She'd hit a nerve with her interest in his family and Ryan was slamming the door in her face.

"Hungry?" she asked.

His dark eyebrows curved inward. "I'm stuffed from lunch."

Tapping her dwindling cash pile, she declared, "If I'm leaning toward bankruptcy, I deserve dessert before I land in jail." She went into the kitchen. Her belly wasn't hungry, just agitated. Probably caused by the mixed signals Ryan had been giving off since he'd shown up on her doorstep earlier this afternoon.

One moment he gazed at her mouth, another he avoided eye contact. He'd brushed her hand with his fingers when he reached for the dice; the next time he'd waited for her to toss them across the board. She didn't need to be a brain scientist to understand he was attracted to her—and didn't want to be.

The box of store-bought cookies on the pantry shelf vied for her attention and she debated whether her hips needed the sweets. Ryan would be the perfect treat. His kiss would satisfy her sugar craving without adding inches to her waistline. The telephone rang, interrupting the *kissing* thoughts. "Hello?"

Joe's panicky voice echoed though the connection. "Oh, no!" she murmured. A moment later Ryan appeared in the kitchen doorway, his expression clouded with concern. For a guy who wanted to be left alone, he appeared at the most interesting times.

"I'll be there as soon as possible." She disconnected the call and explained, "Joe's brother, Willie's, been shot. They've taken him to Queens Hospital Center. I have to go."

"I'll drive you," Ryan offered.

She hated to ask such a favor…but she wanted Ryan by her side. She'd put a lot of energy and time positioning herself in other people's lives, ensuring they could depend on her, that she'd always be around for them. Yet in order to protect her heart, she'd never allowed herself to lean on anyone else. She'd been abandoned by her mother, father, grandmother and aunt. Her heart didn't have the strength to watch another person walk away.

It's just a ride, Anna. "You're positive you have time to drive me to the hospital?"

"Absolutely."

"Let me leave a note for Blair, then I'll grab my purse."

"Don't forget shoes." He nodded to her pink socks.

"Right. Shoes."

Ten minutes later they left the apartment. "You can drop me off at the E.R. doors. I'll catch a ride home from one of Joe's relatives." Anna clutched Ryan's arm as they hurried along the sidewalk. Solid, dependable and by her side—she couldn't ask for anything more than

Ryan at this moment. They rounded the corner and he pointed his key fob at a Lexus. Two bleeps sounded.

"That's your car?" she blurted.

Instead of answering, he held open the passenger-side door. She sank onto the plush leather seat and gawked at the dashboard, which resembled an instrument panel from NASA. Her instincts had been correct. Ryan was definitely an uptown guy. What else besides this car waited for him in Manhattan at the end of each workday?

Uncovering the reasons Ryan was slumming in Queens for a trash company would have to wait. Her main concern at the moment was Joe's fifteen-year-old brother.

"How do I get to the hospital?" Ryan inched the car into traffic.

"East on the Long Island Expressway, then take the Kissena Boulevard exit. The service road leads to 164th Street. Make a right. The hospital isn't far after that."

They drove several minutes in silence, then he asked, "How bad is it?"

"Joe didn't say. Willie was in surgery when Joe called." Surgery was bad. She'd watched the Health Channel enough to understand that if the teen required an operation, he was bleeding internally.

Ryan squeezed her hand. She appreciated that he didn't utter meaningless platitudes—*everything will be okay,* or *don't worry.* She'd heard those utterances all her life from social workers. Most of the time they turned out to be false.

According to the dashboard clock, the drive to the hospital took twenty-seven minutes. He stopped the car in front of the emergency doors. "I'll park, then—"

"You don't have to stay." She searched for the door handle, which appeared to be invisible. "You probably have better things to do."

He leaned across the front seat and opened the door for her. If he had better things to do, he wouldn't have spent an entire afternoon with Anna. An afternoon he'd enjoyed very much—until she'd spotted the Lexus and thrown up a wall between them. Peeved, and maybe a tad offended, he argued, "I'll meet you inside."

Without a word she scrambled from the car and charged into the hospital. If he was smart, he'd wait outside. He wasn't part of Anna's adoptive family. Not that he wanted to be. *Did he?*

When he entered emergency five minutes later, the combined smells of disinfectant, bleach and human body slapped him in the face. The waiting area was noisy and hot. An elderly woman sang to a whimpering baby. Two teens held ice packs to their swollen faces, while a mother ranted at them. A barefoot, homeless man with an oozing gash along his calf slept propped against the vending machine—at least, Ryan hoped he was sleeping, and not dead. He searched for Anna in the crowd.

Her voice reached him. "Over here, Ryan." She stood with Joe in the hallway.

"I'm sorry to hear about your brother." Ryan shook the other man's hand.

"Thanks for bringing Anna. Willie's still in surgery."

"Joe needs a coffee. I'll make a run to the cafeteria." Anna hurried to the elevator.

"Whether my brother lives through surgery or not, he's as good as dead," Joe muttered, then kicked the wall next to him.

"What do you mean?" Ryan was bothered by the sheen in Joe's haunted eyes.

"A gang member came in a few minutes ago asking about Willie."

"They're concerned—"

"They're concerned, all right. Concerned he'll live." Joe snorted. "They want my brother dead."

"You're certain about this?"

"Willie didn't show up for lunch, so my mother sent me looking for him. I checked the basement of an abandoned apartment building, where Willie said the gang meets. As I approached, I heard gunshots, then gangbangers ran out of the building in every direction."

Ryan clenched his jaw. He anticipated how the story would end.

"I found my brother slumped in a corner, shot twice in the gut. They shot him because he'd asked to leave the gang." A tear leaked from the corner of Joe's eye.

Maybe Ryan wasn't as dead inside as he'd believed, because his heart was ripping in two at the sight of the grown man's tears. "Did your brother name the shooter?"

Joe shook his head. "He fell unconscious and never came to, not even when the paramedics arrived."

Rage not dissimilar to what Ryan had experienced after 9/11 filled him and he fought the urge to shake his fist at the heavens and demand someone above the clouds answer for the violence on earth. For the loss of innocent lives.

The elevator doors swooshed open and Anna walked toward them. "Here." She shoved a hot coffee into Joe's hand. "Drink." Then she inquired, "Is Linda here?"

"She's in the waiting room with the others. C'mon." Joe and Anna walked off. After a few steps, Joe glanced over his shoulder. "You coming, Jones?"

The invitation startled Ryan. He wasn't a relative and he wouldn't call himself much of a friend. At his hesitation, Anna held out her hand.

Against his better judgment, Ryan followed. They rode the elevator to the fourth floor, where they entered a private waiting area, packed with family, friends, neighbors and the hospital chaplain.

A middle-aged woman Ryan assumed was Willie's mother rushed to Joe's side. Anna hugged her way around the room, offering sympathy and kind words. Attempting to make himself invisible, Ryan remained by the door, his gaze skirting the curious glances of others. Too many tears. Too many sad faces. Why would a kid turn to a gang, when all this love was his for the taking?

You could ask yourself the same question.

A vision of his grandfather and brothers pacing in a waiting room while he underwent surgery for his burn injuries flashed before Ryan's eyes. He'd been heavily sedated that first week in the hospital, but he'd regained consciousness in snatches, and each time he'd recognized his grandfather or one of his brothers sitting by his bedside. They'd cared. They'd worried. Probably even cried.

And you repaid their love by shutting them out.

9/11 had been a dark, hellish time in his life. He'd permitted his despair to consume him, thus making others miserable. At first, he hadn't realized his depression and anger had affected his family. But as time passed, he'd begun to see the damage his misery had inflicted.

Instead of asking for help, he'd nurtured his rage and resentment, all the while finding a strange comfort in believing he was disappointing his grandfather and weakening his ties with his brothers.

The door at the other end of the room opened and a rumpled, haggard surgeon in bloody scrubs entered. The room went silent—no one dared to breathe. The urge to flee overwhelmed Ryan. He didn't want to be with these grieving people. Most of all, he didn't want to hear the fate of a young boy he'd never met.

"Mr. and Mrs. Smith, I'm sorry."

A gasp. A wail.

"We did everything we could to stop the internal bleeding, but the bullets had done too much damage." The keening grew louder, so the doctor raised his voice. "If you'd care to see your son, follow me."

With a hand on their arms, Joe escorted his parents out the door, and the others lined up to follow. Across the room, Anna's gaze connected with Ryan's. Fat teardrops leaked from her eyes. His own throat swelled. He motioned for her to follow the group.

The door closed, leaving Ryan alone. He sank onto a chair and rested his head in his hands. This friendship thing with Anna was a hell of a lot more than he'd bargained for.

GRAY. COLD. WINDY. The weather a perfect complement to the way Willie's life had ended—ugly.

There was nothing beautiful or warm about putting a fifteen-year-old in the ground and throwing a pile of dirt over his head. Ryan studied Willie's final resting place. The cemetery was old and decrepit, and on the corner of a busy road. Noise and exhaust. Hardly the peaceful plot depicted in movies.

Ryan had bowed out of the visitation at the funeral home last night. He hadn't cared that he'd been the lone person at the station who hadn't attended. He'd seen his share of dead faces during 9/11. He refused to add Willie's to the group that haunted his dreams.

He hadn't wanted to attend the funeral service at the

church this afternoon, either, but Anna and her sweet-talking ways had convinced him to accompany her. He'd picked her up at noon and driven her there. They'd listened to the pastor drone on about God's mercy and forgiveness.

After the service, he and Anna had waited in the parking lot for the casket to be loaded into the hearse. Other family members had cleared the flowers from the church and put them into a car that would transport them to the grave site. His was among the bunch. The biggest. The gaudiest. He didn't know any other way to express his regret over a senseless death, except for the flowers and the obscene amount of money he'd contributed to the station's collection to help the Smiths pay for the funeral expenses.

Now friends congregated, a dark cloud of misery among the masses of funeral flowers, and awaited the arrival of the hearse and the family. Graves with the names *Fleming, Hallstead, Murray, Parker, Becker* eavesdropped on the gathering from the shadows. For Willie's sake, Ryan hoped his new neighbors were nice, caring people.

The crunch of gravel announced the arrival of the hearse. In silence, the pallbearers removed the casket and carried it to the grave site. A second car drove up and the Smith family got out.

Forming a human chain, the parents, Joe and his two younger sisters approached the grave. Joe's father, already ill from a past stroke, withered right before Ryan's eyes. The younger girls wore heavy eye makeup and thrust their chins in the air, determined to appear tougher than the world around them. The mother's empty eyes bothered Ryan the most.

The family sat in chairs in front of the casket and studied the dark hole in the ground. The pastor from the church service recited several Bible verses that glorified death—a bunch of bull, in Ryan's opinion. Death wasn't glorious. It was horrible. And it was permanent.

Ryan closed his eyes and blocked out the religious words. He attempted to retreat to a place in his mind where no one died. No one got hurt. No one got divorced. No one's parents abandoned them. But his conscience refused to grant an escape from the cruel, hard world he lived in.

The brisk wind picked up, whipping hair and coloring noses red. Finally, Willie's mother stood and reached for a handful of dirt from the mound at the foot of the plot. Her bony fingers clung to the soil as if each grain was a piece of her child. The black cloud held its breath, waiting for the brittle white knuckles to release God's newest soul. Joe stepped forward and placed his hand over his mother's. The dirt fell, pinging against the steel casket. The onlookers exhaled, turned and drifted away, leaving the family alone in their final moment of despair.

"I DIDN'T EXPECT to hear from you so soon again," Ryan's grandfather said, after answering the phone.

Ryan shouldn't have called, but he yearned to hear his grandfather's voice. Needed to determine for himself that the old man was alive and well. "I went to a funeral this afternoon."

Silence, then a quiet, "Oh?"

After dropping off Anna at her apartment, Ryan had declined an invitation to come inside. He'd wanted to return to the safety of his self-imposed prison in Manhattan. To an environment he could control. Alone with his thoughts, he'd contemplated his grandfather's mortality and the aging man's number of days left on earth.

The funeral had forced Ryan to admit, with some bewilderment, that he'd been dependent on the McKade patriarch his entire life. He couldn't recall a time or circumstance that he hadn't turned to his grandfather for advice or reassurance. The man had been and remained *the* steadying force in Ryan's life.

"The funeral was for the teenager that had been involved in a gang."

"I'm listening."

"Willie told the gang leader he was quitting. So they shot him."

"I'm sorry, Ryan."

"Grandpa, I can't do this any longer. I tried. For you, I tried. But it's no good." Like Willie, Ryan wanted out. His eyes burned and he cursed Willie and the funeral for leaving him emotionally gutted.

"You want out of what?" his grandfather asked.

"My life lesson—the job at Parnell Brothers. I'd intended to keep my distance and do my time, but no one's leaving me alone. Anna's got me messed up, and I'm playing on their basketball team, and now Willie's dead and I—"

"Hold on, grandson." Ryan clung to the authoritative note in the old man's voice. "Anna who?"

"The company's second-in-command. She's determined to drag me into everyone's life, including hers."

"And that's bad because…?"

"It's not bad, it's…well, it's hard, Grandpa." Becoming involved with Anna and the men at the station had made Ryan vulnerable to his emotions—emotions that he'd stowed deep inside him now bubbled to the surface.

He couldn't figure out how to process all the feelings, and in truth didn't care to, not when he understood only pain.

"Does the woman who's caused this strife have a last name?"

"Nowakowski."

"Quite a mouthful."

"She's a mouthful, all right," Ryan muttered.

"Good kisser, eh?"

Ryan ignored his grandfather's chuckle. "Her kisses are beside the point." How did he explain that Anna's beautiful smile and her laugh caused him pain? Reminded him of what he didn't deserve, what would never be his to cherish?

"Then what *is* your point, Ryan?"

"She wants us to be friends."

"Friendship is a good place to start."

Did he dare admit it? Once spoken, there was no turning back. "I feel more than friendship for her, Grandpa, but I'm worried."

"Of what, my boy?"

"That I'll fall in love." *And then I'll make a wrong move or events beyond my control will take her away from me. Or worse—Anna won't love me back.*

"You're putting the cart before the horse. Enjoy her friendship and don't worry about the future. Trust your heart."

Right then, Call Waiting bleeped. "I've got to get this, Grandpa."

"Stay the course, Ryan. All rough seas eventually calm."

His grandfather hung up and Ryan clicked over to the incoming call. "Hello?"

"It's me, Anna."

His heart stumbled. Had her ears been ringing the entire time he'd discussed her with his grandfather? "Hey," he managed to say.

"I wondered if maybe you'd go out to dinner with me Thursday." *Pause.* "Tomorrow."

He hadn't caught his breath from the funeral and Anna was back in his face. *Tell her no. Make up an excuse.*

"If you're busy, that's okay. But I—"

"I'll go." What happened to *no?* "Should I drive my car in tomorrow?"

"The restaurant's right around the corner from my apartment. We can hop a bus after work."

"Okay."

"Ryan?"

"Yeah?"

"Thanks for rescuing me. I couldn't have made it through the funeral without you," she whispered, her voice catching.

Rescued her? His last attempt at playing Mr. Superhero had resulted in upending his life. *And saving someone else's.* He hadn't considered the consequences of reentering the World Trade Center on 9/11. He'd heard a scream and he'd answered it. The rest was history.

"You're a good friend," she insisted.

He winced at her reminder of the damn friendship clause in their relationship. "See you tomorrow." He hung up. *Dinner with a friend.* He craved more, but did he really believe he could manage an affair…a fling or a one-night stand with Anna, then walk away?

If he hadn't seen the antique portraits hanging on her apartment walls… But he had and they'd touched him.

He wanted to both thank and curse Anna's pretend family for forcing him to acknowledge that his emotional state wasn't a pile of cold ash but smoldering cinders waiting for the right moment—or the right person—to stoke them back to life.

That rainy afternoon in Anna's apartment, Ryan had recognized her need to belong to a family. Since his divorce, he'd suffered from occasional bouts of loneliness but nowhere near the depth that had driven Anna to assemble pretend relatives. He realized the men at Parnell Brothers and their loved ones were as close to a *real* family as Anna would ever have. Whether or not he wished to admit it, Ryan wanted to be a part of that family, too.

But at what cost?

Chapter Eight

Thursday, October 25.

Anna had risen at 6:00 a.m. Made herself breakfast. Caught the bus to the station. Now she waited at her desk for Ryan to shower and change clothes for their dinner date.

But today wasn't just another ordinary day. Eighteen years ago on this very date Anna had given birth to a daughter and had named her Tina. She'd held the baby girl in her arms and had promised to love her for the rest of her life, even though strangers would raise her.

Eyes closed, Anna pictured her daughter's face when she was born—red, pug nose, rosy lips. And eyes so blue the ocean would have been envious. The baby's hair hadn't been Anna's blond color but her birth father's black. Anna had put Michael's name on Tina's birth certificate in case her daughter chose to search for him. Maybe Michael had made a career out of the marines. She hadn't heard from or seen him since she'd informed him he'd gotten her pregnant. Anna had included medical information in Tina's adoption file, as well as a letter from her—the fourteen-year-old mother.

Eighteen years had both flown by and dragged by at

once. Not a day had passed when her daughter hadn't
been in Anna's thoughts. What had Tina asked Santa for
this year? What school did Tina attend? Was she a safe
driver? Was she an honor-roll student? Did she plan to
attend college next fall after she graduated high school
this year? A million questions—but Anna had given up
the right to answers eighteen years ago.

Her daughter's first few birthdays had been difficult
for Anna, still a teenager struggling with her own life
in foster care. She'd walk around malls, searching the
faces of infants and small children, wondering if one of
them was Tina. The little information the social worker
had offered Anna was that a family living somewhere
in NYC had adopted Tina. Anna had been comforted in
believing her daughter was nearby.

Not that her daughter's location mattered as much
now. Tina could be halfway around the world and it
wouldn't change the fact that her daughter's image and
the sound of her cry remained nestled in Anna's heart.
She remembered 9/11 and the panic she'd experienced,
wondering if Tina or her parents had been caught in that
disaster. Anna had phoned the social worker who'd
handled her daughter's adoption and begged her to find
out if Tina was okay. The caseworker had called back
the next day with the news that Tina and her family were
fine and hadn't been anywhere near the Twin Towers.

That tragic event had convinced Anna there would
never be a moment in her life she wouldn't worry or
wonder about her child. Giving birth to a child was an
event you couldn't put behind you. An experience you
couldn't pretend had never happened. Tina would
always be a part of Anna. Because of that, Anna decided
that tonight she would tell Ryan about her daughter.

If Anna hoped to pursue a long-term relationship with Ryan, there could be no secrets between them. After Willie's funeral Anna had decided that she didn't want to go through the rest of her life always being available to other people but never depending on anyone. For the first time in forever she'd reached out, and Ryan had been there for her. He'd made her realize she didn't always have to be the strong one. That it was okay to lean on another person.

Her heart insisted she could make him happy. He could make her happy. But first she had to risk everything and tell him the truth about Tina.

Ryan had lost a child of his own, but that hadn't been his fault. No, a cruel act of nature he couldn't have prevented had stolen his child from him. Would Ryan understand Anna hadn't had any choice in giving up her baby? Or would he believe she'd taken the coward's way out?

"Ready?" Ryan stood in the doorway, wearing khaki slacks and a black crew-neck sweater, his leather bomber jacket slung over one shoulder.

With a little effort she found a smile for him. He deserved that and more for agreeing to dinner tonight. The afternoon Willie had died, Anna had noticed a change in Ryan. He talked less. Joked less. Smiled less. Little by little he was withdrawing from her and the men. Anna had already lost so much in her life—her parents, her daughter, Bobby's brother, Willie, and now Ryan was slipping away.

"You look nice," she commented as she approached. *And you smell good, too.* He'd splashed cologne on in the locker room and the earthy scent made her want to rub her big nose against his clean-shaven cheek and inhale until she was high on Ryan.

Ever the gentlemen, he retrieved her coat from the rack by the door and held it up so she could slip her arms inside. "I hope you enjoy Italian."

"Mimi's again?" he asked.

Mimi's was too loud for the talk she planned to have with him. "DiRisio's. They have a wonderful wine selection and their spaghetti and meatballs are to die for."

As they walked the two blocks to the bus stop, Ryan grumbled, "I should have driven my car into the city today."

"What's the matter? You don't like buses?" She grinned at his eye roll. When they reached the bus stop, she checked her watch—three minutes to fill with conversation. "How did Joe act today?"

"Kept to himself."

Bobby had encouraged Joe to take as much time as he needed before coming back to the job. But Joe had arrived bright and early this morning. He'd insisted he had to get out of the house—away from his mother's crying and his father's silence.

"I wish Joe would seek grief counseling." Anna's social worker had forced her to submit to counseling after she'd given Tina away. The first few sessions Anna had been angry and sad and had refused to talk. Then one session the nice lady had handed Anna a picture of a baby wrapped in a pink blanket and Anna had believed that baby in the photo was Tina. She'd burst out crying and had sobbed in the woman's arms the entire session. When the tears had dried, she'd talked. Talking hadn't chased the hurt away, but Anna had learned the importance of dealing with her emotions rather than keeping them bottled up.

The bus crawled alongside the curb. They hopped on

The Harlequin Reader Service® — Here's how it works:

If offer card is missing write to: Harlequin Reader Service, 3010 Walden Ave., P.O. Box 1867, Buffalo NY 14240-1867

BUSINESS REPLY MAIL
FIRST-CLASS MAIL   PERMIT NO. 717-003   BUFFALO, NY

POSTAGE WILL BE PAID BY ADDRESSEE

HARLEQUIN READER SERVICE
3010 WALDEN AVE
PO BOX 1867
BUFFALO NY 14240-9952

NO POSTAGE
NECESSARY
IF MAILED
IN THE
UNITED STATES

and chose a seat in the middle. A teen in front of them blasted his iPod. A baby cried in the back and two men nearby engaged in a heated debate about the New York Giants football team. As the bus drove away from the curb, Ryan threaded his fingers through hers and held her hand against his thigh.

Today had been difficult for everyone at the station. More than ever, Anna appreciated the warmth of Ryan's touch. A block from the restaurant they got off the bus. "DiRisio's is right around the corner," she announced.

Hand in hand they arrived at the small family-owned restaurant.

"Anna, my love, where have you been?" Isabella DiRisio hugged Anna as soon as she and Ryan walked through the door.

"I've missed you, too," Anna consoled the older woman with iron-gray hair. "Isabella, meet Ryan Jones. He works at Parnell Brothers."

Ryan offered his hand, but Isabella brushed his fingers aside and clasped his face between her meaty fingers. After kissing both cheeks, she smiled. "It is good that Anna has a man now. Come. I take you to the back."

They followed Isabella to a table in a dark corner. Isabella lit the candle in the centerpiece, then scurried off. A minute later she appeared with a basket of warm bread and a carafe of red wine. "No menus tonight. Enrico will prepare a feast." She kissed her fingertips and waltzed into the kitchen.

"A feast?" Ryan remained starry-eyed. Isabella had that effect on people.

"Enrico is Isabella's husband and the chef." Before Anna could add anything else, the couple appeared at the table.

"I told you." Isabella patted Ryan's shoulder. "Our Anna has a date tonight."

"Hello, Enrico. May I introduce you to Ryan Jones. Ryan…Enrico."

The men shook hands, then the rotund chef announced, "I will prepare a meal for the lovers."

And so the evening progressed, with Isabella delivering food and refilling their wineglasses and Enrico stopping by their table every ten minutes to inquire if they enjoyed each dish. Anna had lost count of the number of times she and Ryan had to restart their discussion.

"Do you remember much about your childhood, Ryan?" she asked when Isabella had delivered their desserts and had finally left them in peace.

"I don't have any memories of my parents. But I had a good life with my grandfather and brothers. Why?"

Did she have to have a reason to learn more about him? "I dreamed of being raised in one house by one family."

"Tell me about Charlie," he said. "What kinds of things did you two do?"

My, my, my. Ryan was an expert at steering the topic away from himself. At the rate they were going she'd never get up the nerve to engage in a dialogue about her daughter.

"Charlie worked at a fast-food restaurant as soon as school got out in the afternoons, until ten o'clock at night. Although we lived in the same house, I didn't see him a whole lot. When he was home, we played basketball in the driveway or threw the football around. I wasn't any good at sports, but I was always willing to play. Charlie bragged I'd make a good brother."

"I've never met a woman as comfortable around men as you are."

The comment caught her by surprise. "Men are easy to get along with." *Most, anyway.* "They don't keep secrets the way women do." *Like me.* Anna reached for her wineglass, drained the last few swallows, then announced, "I have a secret."

Before Anna drew another breath, Isabella joined them at the table. "Now we talk."

So much for coming clean about her daughter tonight.

Isabella took Ryan's hand and placed it atop Anna's on the table. "Tell Isabella...what are your intentions toward my Anna?"

Lord, she loved Isabella and Enrico. They were caring people who meant well and were determined to find a suitable husband for Anna. But Ryan would be lucky if he escaped tonight without having to propose to her.

"Ryan, got a minute?" Anna hovered near the locker-room door, a tired smile curving her lips. Willie's death lingered in everyone's minds and a week after the funeral the mood at the station remained somber.

"What's up?" he asked.

"Actually, I have a couple of things I need to talk to you about." The subtle scent of her perfume drifted past his nose, and he wondered if he'd ever have the chance to discover for himself where on her body she spritzed the fragrance. Behind her ears...the pulse at the base of her throat...her wrists...between her breasts?

A quick check of the wall clock told him the other men, even Leon, had left for the night. No one stuck around past quitting time on Fridays.

"How's work going at the Blackwell factory?" She moved about the room, checking the air fresheners.

Anna was nervous. She'd been edgy since their dinner date at DiRisio's last Thursday.

Friday morning following their dinner, he'd expected Anna to confess the big secret she'd intended to tell him before Isabella's interruption. Instead, Anna had avoided him, and continued to do so all this week—which made her appearance in the locker room right now suspicious.

"We'll finish the job Tuesday. Wednesday at the latest." Ryan doubted Anna was interested in how many loads of garbage they'd hauled from the condemned factory near the railroad tracks.

She nibbled her lower lip, a nervous habit he considered cute. "You've been quiet lately. Is everything all right?"

He'd been quiet? What about her? "I'm fine," he growled.

Tears welled in her blue eyes, and before Ryan could stop himself, he'd crossed the room and pulled Anna into his arms. She snuggled her head under his chin, and he lowered his face and breathed in the fresh scent of her soft hair. Her warm, curvy body felt good...right, pressed against him. "I'm sorry I snapped. It's been a long week." *All I've thought about is you, and how to fit into your world.*

She rubbed her nose against the front of his T-shirt. "You're a special man, Ryan Jones."

Each time she spoke his last name he was reminded of who he really was—a McKade. Not a Jones. Not a man who worked with his hands for a living, but a rich man who hid from life. Uncomfortable with her praise, he insisted, "What did you want to talk about?" He should have kept his mouth shut. As soon as he asked the question, she wiggled free and paced the floor.

"It's Bobby."

"The boss?" Now that Anna mentioned the man, Ryan realized he hadn't seen Parnell since the funeral. "What about him?"

"He's behaving oddly. Make that has been behaving oddly since he and his wife separated."

"I wasn't aware he was having marital problems."

"He and Mary separated once before, right after his brother, Harold, passed away."

This wasn't any of his business, but after almost two months on the job, Anna probably considered *him* family now. "What kind of odd behavior?"

"When Bobby's in his office, he's always on the phone."

"And that's unusual because…?"

"He shuts the door. He's never done that."

"Maybe he wants privacy."

"I don't think so." Her mouth formed a thin line. "I stumbled upon a glitch in the accounting books."

That didn't sound good. "What kind of glitch?"

"The numbers don't balance. Money is vanishing right under my nose, which is unusual considering its size."

His lips curved in a semblance of a smile. "Have you told the boss?"

"I brought up the missing money before Willie's funeral and he got a funny expression on his face, then mumbled an excuse and left the office."

A sad sigh escaped Anna, the sound tugging at Ryan's heart. "You know where the money's going, don't you," he said.

"He's gambling again," she whispered.

"Again?"

"That's why Mary left him the first time. Bobby

began betting after Harold's death. Mary got him into counseling and their marriage survived."

There was no fast, simple cure for a gambling addiction. Rolling the dice or betting at the track was an emotional sickness that a person had to manage his or her entire life. Ryan remembered the boss calling him into his office to ask his intentions toward Anna. Ryan had noticed the desktop littered with newspapers opened to the sports page. Bobby bet on sports teams. "Didn't you mention the boss had gone to Atlantic City when Willie was shot?" He refrained from using the word *killed.* No one at the station ever said Willie had been killed. Or murdered. Those words were too final. Everyone continued to use the word *shot*—as if that word would somehow keep the teen's death from becoming real.

"Actually, Bobby said he was headed to Forty-first Street and Eighth Avenue."

"What gave you the idea he went to Atlantic City?"

"The address I just mentioned is where the Port Authority Terminal is located. Buses leave every hour for Atlantic City." She rubbed her brow. "I did something I shouldn't have."

Ryan swallowed a groan. Was this the big secret she'd planned to confess last week at DiRisio's? He'd changed his mind. He didn't want to hear any more. The less he knew, the less involved he'd become—although Anna appeared determined to drag him into everyone's problems. "What did you do, Anna?"

"We usually receive payments for our services around the first of the month. But this past Wednesday a check came in. Instead of depositing the money into the company bank account, I opened a second account for the business under my name and deposited the money. Without that check I wouldn't have been able to meet payroll and the guys would have gone home with empty pockets."

"Aren't you putting your job on the line?" He hoped the men appreciated Anna's loyalty.

"Bobby won't be happy when he finds out, but he won't fire me."

"What can I do?" *Damn.* Sticking his nose in places he shouldn't.

"Did you drive your car in to work today?" When he nodded, she pleaded, "Help me find Bobby."

"Where do you want to begin searching?"

"Atlantic City. I phoned Mary this afternoon. She filed for divorce and Bobby moved out two weeks ago. He's been staying with friends and Mary hasn't seen or heard from him since."

Oh, hell. What else did he have to do this weekend besides sit alone in his bedroom and watch TV. "Fine. We'll stop at your apartment so you can pack a change of clothes, then we'll head over to mine."

"I brought an overnight bag to work with me."

Surprised, he asked, "Were you planning to go to Atlantic City alone if I'd refused?"

"Maybe," she hedged, a wry smile tilting the corners of her mouth.

Yep, she was stubborn enough to travel by herself if she had to. Ryan didn't cotton to the idea of Anna searching for Parnell among the thugs and street scum who lurked outside the casinos.

"I owe you big-time, Ryan." She went up on tiptoe and pressed her mouth to his. Soft. Featherlight. When she shifted away, he swore he read a promise in those blue eyes. What that promise meant he hadn't a clue. But he was willing to gamble it had to do with sin.

Caesars Palace, here we come.

"YOU LIVE IN THE—" Anna dipped her head to peer out the passenger-side window at the letters carved into the stone facade "—Klinedore Building?"

Ryan didn't respond to the question. Instead, he strangled the steering wheel and gazed out the windshield. Maybe he hadn't heard her. "When did they convert the building into apartments?"

"They didn't." Still no eye contact. "I live on the thirtieth floor. The rest of the building is office space."

He lived on a whole floor? She yearned to ask how he'd arranged that but feared he'd blurt out an outrageous answer—such as he owned the whole building. Impossible. *Is it?*

Okay. She admitted that, when she first met Ryan, she'd suspected him of being an uptown guy. The Lexus, the two thousand dollars in the collection jar for Willie's funeral expenses and now the Klinedore Building…all confirmed her earlier suspicion. She exhaled a silent sigh at the realization that she and Ryan were literally worlds apart. Ryan had been the first man in years to pique her interest and wiggle his way into her heart. She'd been hoping… *For what? A white wedding?*

There was much more between her and Ryan than a couple of kisses, a game of Monopoly, a funeral and a dinner at DiRisio's. She believed Ryan was physically attracted to her, although she sensed he didn't wish to be. She prided herself on reading other people, but same as her, Ryan harbored secrets.

"A man is standing next to my door. Should I see what he wants?" she asked.

"That's Waldo, the doorman." Ryan's brown-eyed gaze swung her way, and she swore he winced.

Stung, she snapped, "If you'd rather I stay here…" Darn it, she didn't care to wait in the car. She wanted to check out Ryan's apartment. Sneak a peek inside his world. Find out personal tidbits about him—the color of his bath towels. Did he have leather or fabric sofas? What kind of artwork decorated the walls? Did he leave his toothbrush out on the counter or put it in the medicine cabinet?

"Come on." He waved a hand at Waldo, who immediately leaned forward and opened Anna's door.

"Good evening, ma'am." He helped her from the car.

Although she wore a long jean skirt, leather boots and a nice sweater, she was underdressed for Manhattan. "Thank you, Waldo." She flashed a warm smile.

"Sir." Waldo nodded to Ryan, then walked ahead and held open the lobby door.

"We'll be out in ten minutes." A hand on her elbow, Ryan escorted Anna to a bank of elevators. She quickened her pace, fearing that if she asked him to slow down, he'd send her back to the car. As if by magic, the elevator farthest on the right opened. After they entered and the door closed, Ryan kept his back to her, his hands curling and uncurling at his sides. Obviously, he was uncomfortable bringing her to his apartment. Why? She found it difficult to believe a man as handsome as Ryan hadn't brought a woman home after his divorce. She wished she had a crystal ball and could see into the future—hers and Ryan's. The more she learned about him, the more she worried if she was setting herself up for heartache.

The elevator stopped, and as soon as the doors opened, Ryan bolted. Anna hesitated, apprehensive about what surprises awaited her behind the double mahogany doors across the foyer.

"Change your mind?" His hard stare challenged her, as if he sensed she was poised to run.

C'mon, Anna. Don't be a chicken. She left the elevator and entered his apartment. Approximately three steps inside, she froze. The room was empty. No furniture. No artwork. No lamps. Not even a rug covered the tile floor.

"Be right back." His announcement bounced off the barren walls and she jumped inside her skin. After he disappeared, she sucked in a lungful of air, startled she'd been holding her breath.

Ryan's home was nothing more than an empty box. Stark whiteness with ornate moldings and floor-to-ceiling windows overlooking the bay. Her eyes burned at the thought of Ryan standing alone in front of the dark glass walled off from the world outside.

The kitchen was to the left of the living area. Stainless steel appliances and granite countertops. She didn't have to snoop inside the refrigerator to figure out the contents—water bottles, maybe leftover Chinese takeout and a few condiments. If not for the coffee-maker on the counter and the ceramic mug next to it, she'd assume the kitchen had never been used.

The crushing weight of the loneliness and grief filling Ryan's apartment threatened to smother her, as if an anvil rested on her chest. What had happened to reduce him to this desolate existence? Had he loved his wife so much he couldn't go on without her?

When she envisioned a future with Ryan, she

cringed. Add her hang-ups from a childhood spent in foster care to the baggage from his marriage and the two of them together spelled disaster.

Anna spun in a slow circle and noticed built-in book-cases on either side of the front entry. Save for one, the shelves were empty. Intrigued by the novels toppled on their sides, she moved closer, intent on discovering Ryan's reading preferences.

The books were classics. *The Old Man and the Sea. To Kill a Mockingbird. The Grapes of Wrath. Moby Dick.* She was about to move away, when an object caught her eye. On tiptoe, she reached behind the books. A picture frame.

A photo of a beautiful woman. Ryan's wife? Upon closer inspection, Anna noticed the photograph had been torn in several places, then taped together. This woman had caused Ryan much pain and grief. Ryan was a good man. An honest man. A man with integrity. He didn't deserve whatever it was that this woman had done to him. She returned the picture to the shelf.

Her thoughts drifted to Atlantic City. She'd be a liar if she didn't admit that she hoped this weekend might turn romantic between her and Ryan. She might not be as beautiful as Ryan's ex, but she cared about him more. Besides, foster care had taught Anna to be a fighter. And she just happened to believe Ryan was worth fighting for.

Ryan returned to the living room. He'd changed into casual dress pants and wore a suit coat over an olive-colored turtleneck sweater—handsome and sophisticated. "Ready?" he asked.

"All set." She waited for him to make a move toward the door, but he hesitated. *Please don't change your mind.* "If you'd rather not go, I'll catch a bus to Atlantic City." She didn't want to ride in a stinky, crowded bus. She preferred to ride in Ryan's comfortable Lexus.

He carried his overnight bag across the room and set it at her feet. Tenderly, he touched her cheek. "For better or worse, I'm along for the ride."

Chapter Nine

"If it's all right with you, I intend to search at least one casino before finding a room for the night." Anna studied the flashing neon lights as Ryan drove south on Atlantic Avenue.

The dashboard clock read nine-thirty. Ryan was bushed after a full day of garbage detail with Antonio and Patrick, but he couldn't ignore the hopeful note in Anna's voice. "Which casino did you have in mind?"

"The Borgata."

"Why that hotel?" he asked.

"I phoned Mary earlier to tell her I planned to go to Atlantic City to search for Bobby."

Ryan wondered if the boss's wife deemed it odd that the company secretary was out searching for her husband. Then he recalled how Anna had claimed the employees at Parnell Brothers were one big, happy family—one big, happy, *dysfunctional* family. Ryan considered himself the worst one in the bunch.

"A while back, Mary discovered a deck of cards from the Borgata in Bobby's dresser drawer. A matchbook with the casino logo turned up in his trouser pocket."

A deck of cards. A matchbook. What did Ryan

possess that would expose his weaknesses? Save for the photograph of his ex-wife, he could think of nothing. Unless one believed *nothing* evidence. When Sandra left him, he'd demanded she take all their possessions—furniture, dishes, towels, bedsheets, artwork. Everything. He'd desired no reminders of the life they'd shared.

After the divorce was final, he'd discovered the picture of his wife in a kitchen drawer. Whether she'd left it intentionally or not, he didn't care. He'd torn it up. Then the next morning he'd confiscated the pieces of her image from the wastebasket and painstakingly glued them together. He'd decided he needed at least one reminder of what they'd shared—the loss of their unborn child. Ryan shook off the memories and followed the signs for valet parking at the Borgata.

The attendant opened Anna's door. Ryan suppressed a grin at her wide-eyed expression as she sized up the thug waiting to assist her. Ryan exited the car, slipped the man a twenty, then reached for Anna's hand. He squeezed her fingers reassuringly and hoped for her sake they'd discover Parnell at one of the blackjack or craps tables.

"Have you ever been in this casino?" he asked after they'd entered the polished marble lobby.

"No. I visited Atlantic City with a friend several years ago but never came in here."

"Check out the chandelier." He indicated the colorful work of art near the bank of elevators.

"It's beautiful." Anna craned her neck as they walked toward the entrance to the gaming area.

"Dale Chihuly is a master glassblower. His creations illuminate several public areas in the hotel." He pulled

Anna to a stop and studied the layout of the floor. Finding Parnell wouldn't be easy in the 125,000-square-foot place.

"Wow." Anna rotated in a circle.

"Over thirty-five hundred slots and over one hundred sixty gaming tables."

Anna's shoulders slumped in defeat. "We'll never find him."

"We will if he's here. You begin with the slots and I'll check the tables and catch up with you in an hour."

She snagged his coat sleeve. "Thank you, Ryan."

Those big blue eyes wielded the power to make him do almost anything. "Watch your purse," he warned.

An hour later he spotted Anna showing a casino-lounge waitress a photograph of Parnell. The scantily clad woman shook her head, then slipped away to deliver drinks to a rowdy group of men. "Any luck?" he asked Anna as he approached.

"No. You?"

"He's not here." Ryan had questioned several dealers and not one recalled Parnell sitting at their table.

"We have to find him." Anna's voice shook with worry and fatigue.

"The odds of locating Parnell this weekend aren't in our favor. He might be holed up drunk somewhere in a dingy motel off the Boardwalk." Ryan shoved a hand through his hair. The man deserved to sit and rot for what he was putting Anna through.

And what about you, Ryan? Are you any better than Parnell for what you put your family through after 9/11?

That's different. I didn't choose to attack my country. I didn't choose to get injured. I was the victim, damn it!

Frustrated, he snapped, "Anna, Parnell's got big problems. You finding him won't solve them."

"If you feel that way, then why did you come with me?"

Tell her the truth. She deserves at least that from you.

"Because it's dangerous for a woman all alone in Atlantic City." *Liar.* He neglected to mention that he was hoping to sleep with her.

"You're right. We'll never find him." Tears flooded her eyes. "Let's go."

Aw, damn. Now he'd snatched her hope. "We might run across a casino dealer who's spotted him."

She nibbled away the remainder of her lipstick, then covered her mouth and yawned. Purple smudges beneath her eyes testified to her exhaustion.

"C'mon. Let's check in to a room and grab some shut-eye." He stroked his thumb across her chin. "We'll search again in the morning. If he's here, we'll find him. I promise."

"But—"

"No buts." If given the choice, Anna would prowl the gaming halls until all hours of the morning. Someone had to watch over her. Might as well be him. With an arm around her shoulders, he escorted her through the lobby. When had it become necessary for him to shelter this woman from hurt? From pain? From the unfairness of life?

While they waited outside for the valet to fetch the Lexus, Anna suggested, "There's a Holiday Inn on the Boardwalk."

"We're staying at the Trump Plaza."

"Trump Plaza? The rooms are too expensive," she argued.

"I get a special deal when I stay at the Plaza," he

admitted. If Anna discovered McKade Import-Export paid three times her annual salary to reserve a year-round suite at the Plaza for business purposes, she'd pass out on the sidewalk.

"I doubt I could afford a room even with your special deal."

Ignoring her protest, he tipped the attendant, helped Anna into the Lexus and drove to the hotel, where he parked in a reserved spot in the underground garage.

"I'm covering the bill," he stated, getting out of the car.

"I'll pay you back in installments—" she dug in her purse and removed fifty dollars, then held the cash out to him "—starting with this."

If he didn't accept the money, she'd argue all night. The last thing he wanted to do was fight. Without comment, he slipped the money into his pants pocket, then removed their bags from the trunk. They rode the elevator to the main lobby. When the doors opened, Ryan suggested, "Why don't you check the menu at the restaurant in the lounge. We may want to order a meal from room service."

Ryan went to the front desk alone.

"Good evening, Mr. McKade," James, the night manager, greeted him. "It's been a while since we've had the pleasure of your company, sir."

Over a year, if Ryan's memory served correct. "Evening, James."

"After you phoned earlier, I sent maid service to freshen up your rooms."

"Thank you." Ryan glanced over his shoulder. Anna was engaged in a discussion with a couple leaving the restaurant. "I have a guest staying with me."

"Yes, sir."

"And, James, call me Jones. Ryan *Jones*."

The desk manager didn't blink an eye. "As you wish…Mr. Jones."

"Ready?" Anna approached, offering a tired smile to the desk clerk.

James slid two key cards onto the counter. "Enjoy your stay, and please don't hesitate to contact the front desk if you require further assistance."

Ryan carried the luggage to the elevator. When the door closed behind them, Anna asked, "What floor are we on?"

"The top." He didn't tell her the suite overlooked the Boardwalk. She must be starving. He was. They'd grabbed a snack at a gas station before leaving New York City, but that was five hours ago. "Does the restaurant in the lobby appeal to you?"

"Too expensive. Besides, I hate snails, oysters…anything that lives in a shell."

With midnight around the corner, taking Anna somewhere nice, along the lines of Roberto's on the sixth floor, was out of the question. "We'll order room service." The doors opened onto their floor and Ryan inserted the key card into the lock.

Hoping Anna wouldn't fuss over the luxurious accommodations, he put her overnight bag in the master suite and his things in the smaller bedroom at the end of the hall. When he returned to the living room, he found her gazing out the window at the Boardwalk. With the cold evening air and brisk wind off the ocean, no one but die-hard gamblers dared move about at night.

Sliding his hands around Anna's waist, he rested his chin on her head. A trace of perfume lingered on her skin and he breathed deeply. He longed to sleep with Anna. To share a bed with her. She had the perfect body for snuggling—soft and curvy in all the right places. No sharp elbows or bony hips to jar a man awake. Tonight he'd have to settle for dreaming about sleeping with her.

He studied her reflection in the glass, watching her take inventory of the room—the velvet wallpaper that matched the material on the sofas, the plasma TV above the fireplace. The kitchenette and bar area. Her gaze stalled on the bottle of champagne Ryan assumed James had sent up with the maids.

"What are you hungry for?" He brushed a strand of hair from her cheek, allowing his fingers to linger against the delicate skin at her temple.

"Macaroni and cheese sounds good." She shifted in his arms and rested her cheek against his sweater, then yawned. Ryan's chest swelled with emotion—with a sentiment he refused to name.

They were staying at a Trump hotel and she wanted macaroni and cheese? God, she could be so damn cute without even trying. "You unpack and I'll phone in our order."

"Fine." She rolled onto her toes, her mouth aiming for his cheek. He turned his face at the last second and their lips connected. He kept the kiss light, gentle. He didn't want to pressure her into making love until they'd talked. Until she agreed to a simple, no-strings-attached weekend affair. Because that was all this could be.

"I'm going to get ready for bed while we wait for the food." She nipped his lower lip, then waltzed off.

After phoning room service, Ryan collapsed on the couch and wondered what Anna thought of the expensive suite.

Why hadn't his grandfather or, for that matter, his elder brother, Nelson, challenged him on this foolish waste of money? Had they feared that if they'd confronted him, he'd retreat deeper into his shell? When had his family become afraid for him? Or worse, had his selfish behavior alienated his family to the point where they no longer cared what he did?

His throat swelled with shame. Keeping the suite allowed Ryan to pretend his life had returned to normal after 9/11, when in fact it hadn't. The Lexus, the empty apartment, the hotel—all signs of a *pretend*-normal life.

Had his grandfather been correct? Was Ryan a coward? Afraid to trust? Afraid to risk his heart again? Just plain afraid of living?

Maybe he pretended with his life, but he wasn't pretending with Anna—was he? He closed his eyes and rested his head against the cushion.

Knock, knock. Startled, Ryan popped off the couch, then stood for a moment battling a wave of light-headedness. He answered the door and the hotel employee rolled the cart into the room. Ryan handed him a tip, then hurried him out.

Stomach rumbling, he went to fetch Anna, but found her sound asleep on the bed. She hadn't even changed into her pajamas. Sweet and innocent, she rested her cheek on one hand, her face relaxed as if she hadn't a care in the world. He didn't have the heart to wake her. He removed a blanket from the closet and tucked it around her, then went back to the living room, where he lifted the covers off the dishes and sniffed.

Instead of having Anna as he'd hoped, he'd have to make do with her macaroni and cheese.

RYAN STEPPED OUT of the shower and knotted a plush hotel towel around his waist. Then he rubbed a hand towel over his wet hair and tossed the towel into the tub.

His stomach rumbled as he thought about the coffee and pastries he'd ordered for breakfast.

After wiping the steamy mirror, he lathered his face with shaving cream. Rinse. Drag. Rinse. Drag. He'd finished one cheek when Anna's panicky voice carried down the hall.

"Ryan? Ryan, are you okay?"

The blade hovered above his skin, his gaze glued to the bathroom mirror. He began to speak but a second later the door burst open. Mussed hair, swollen eyes and a sleep crease along her cheek, Anna, soft and cuddly in the morning, barged into the room.

Soft and cuddly gave way to rigid and detached. As if the moment unfolded in slow motion, Ryan witnessed Anna's surprised expression alter to horror when her gaze connected with his naked back and shoulder. She slapped a hand over her mouth, and he waited for her to vomit.

A surreal fog closed around him as Anna's image in the mirror transformed into his ex-wife's face. How could he have been so stupid, naive, to expect that Anna's reaction to his imperfect body would be different from his ex-wife's? He'd hoped Anna would see beyond the puckering flesh and missing muscle—unlike Sandra, who hadn't been able to stand the sight of his scars, let alone touch them. Evidently, he didn't know Anna as well as he'd assumed. The realization pained him more than the disgust in her eyes.

Then Anna's gaze connected with his in the mirror. "I'm sorry. I thought…"

He winced at her struggle to swallow. He yearned to comfort her. To assure her that her response was normal. To insist everything was fine. But the words became clogged in his throat.

Forcing a calm he didn't feel, he commanded, "Shut the door."

"I...I—"

"Anna. Please leave."

"Sorry," she mumbled as she fled the room. The door closed with a quiet, ear-shattering *click*. Bracing his hands on either side of the sink, Ryan hung his head. From now on Anna would tiptoe around him. Act as though she hadn't seen his scars. And her already too-bright smile would blind him the next time she flashed it.

Damn. Now he had no chance of a weekend affair. Anna was the first woman in longer than he could remember who'd awakened his body. Made him feel alive. Made him want to be intimate with a woman. *Shit. Shit. Shit.* Swearing didn't help anything, but it made him feel better.

Ten minutes later, he'd finished shaving and dressing. He grabbed his wallet. He needed time—alone. And Anna needed time to come to grips with what she'd seen in the bathroom. They would both be better off splitting up when they searched for Parnell. When he left his bedroom, he heard the shower running in Anna's suite. He jotted down his cell phone number and a quick note telling her that he'd search for Parnell in the casinos and she should concentrate her efforts along the Boardwalk. Then he propped the note against the coffeepot, grabbed his keys and slipped out.

ANNA WASN'T POSITIVE how long she'd been sitting on a bench outside the oldest remaining Ripley's Believe It or Not Museum on the Boardwalk when a shadow fell across her feet. The brown loafers looked familiar. With a heavy heart she lifted her head.

Hands in his pockets, face somber, Ryan studied the whitecaps dancing across the ocean. He sported a maroon turtleneck beneath a tweed jacket. A handsome outfit. No one would guess that his perfect clothes hid an imperfect body. She suspected the material concealed more than old injuries—the fabric hid a bruised and battered soul.

He stood. She sat. Neither spoke. Then Ryan cleared his throat. "How long have you been here?"

A check of her watch confirmed several hours. "Most of the morning."

A quick nod, then he glanced away, as if making eye contact was too painful. *Can you blame him? For mercy's sake, you almost threw up at the sight of his scars.*

"Have you had lunch?" he asked.

"No." She hadn't eaten breakfast, either. As a result of her behavior this morning she'd lost her appetite.

"You should eat."

Tears burned her eyes. She didn't deserve his concern. Sniffling, she rubbed a finger under her nose. "I'm not hungry."

After a long moment, he expelled a haggard breath. "Move over."

The bench was small, and his thigh rubbed hers. Anna struggled to find the words to apologize for her inexcusable behavior. *I'm sorry* seemed…trite. Cold.

A thorough analysis of her reaction in the bathroom brought her to one conclusion: she had deep feelings for Ryan. Why else would her heart have wept at the sight of his wounded flesh?

Anna's heart had been vulnerable to Ryan since the moment he'd arrived to work at Parnell Brothers. He unnerved her, yet he steadied her. How could a man do these two things at once? It didn't matter that Ryan wasn't who he'd claimed to be. She'd connected with the real Ryan—the one who wouldn't let the world see his scars.

Ryan had supported her when Willie had been shot. He was here now searching for Bobby because of her. When she'd caught a glimpse of the horrific damage to his body, all of a sudden her heart had doubled in size. That moment she'd understood with crystal-clear clarity that her feelings for Ryan Jones had surpassed attraction and caring—she'd fallen in love with him.

Yes, love. For better or worse. For good or bad. Anastazia Nowakowski had fallen head over heels for Ryan Jones.

Leaning forward, Ryan rested his forearms on his thighs and clasped his hands between his knees. "I was injured during 9/11."

A gasp of blood-chilling shock raced up her throat. Determined to control her emotions, she clamped her lips together. Of all the scenarios her mind had conjured, the World Trade Center attack had not been one of them. She'd imagined a fiery car crash. A backyard-barbecue accident. A camping fire. Never a September 11 story.

She'd met several people who'd lived to tell of that horrific event. Anna shouldn't be surprised Ryan had been touched by the same tragedy that had maimed or killed thousands of people.

Even after six years, the terror remained fresh in her memory. She'd viewed the horrors unfold on the TV in Bobby's office and had suffered shock, dismay, then anger that her neighbors, her city, her country, had been so viciously attacked. She'd worried about her daughter and cried for hours as she witnessed her fellow New

Yorkers race through smoke-choked streets, dodging debris and breathing in poisonous ash.

Ryan survived, Anna.

"Tell me. I want to understand," she whispered after a prolonged silence.

"I was in a meeting in the North Tower that morning. Sixteenth floor. When all hell broke loose, we ran for the exits. The stairwells were jammed with people…screaming, crying, shoving and stumbling over one another. I made it to the lobby."

The words didn't come easy and Anna sensed Ryan hadn't spoken about the past to anyone in a long time—if ever.

"When I exited the building, I tripped and landed on my knees. People swarmed around me and it was impossible to get to my feet. I crawled to the curb and stood. I made the mistake of glancing up. I saw a body floating to the ground, light as a feather. At first my brain didn't put it together. Then two people holding hands jumped from another window. The sky rained people."

Anna closed her eyes and swallowed the bile rising in her throat.

"Sirens were blaring, alarms going off. Helicopters hovered overhead." He rubbed his brow. "I shouldn't have been able to hear that woman's scream." Ryan's eyes connected with Anna's, pleading for an explanation—anything to help him understand.

Tears leaked from Anna's eyes. Useless tears. Tears that couldn't heal Ryan's wounds. Couldn't erase that fateful day in history. She clasped his hand, and instead of pulling away as she feared, he tightened his grip around her fingers.

"I followed the scream and went back into the

building. The woman was pinned near the stairwell. No one had stopped to help her. I managed to free her, but she couldn't stand. I picked her up. Before I got to the doors, I heard an explosion. Heat seared my jacket, but I stumbled outside with the woman." He shuddered. "A paramedic took her. The next thing I remember was waking up in the E.R."

No doubt in agonizing pain. "Oh, Ryan. You were so lucky to make it out of the tower alive."

His glacial stare chilled her. "Was I, Anna?"

Chapter Ten

Hell. Ryan should have kept his mouth shut.

The stunned expression on Anna's face sent a white-hot pang of regret through him. If she hadn't already suspected, then his remark confirmed he carried plenty of baggage from 9/11.

"The first year following the attack was difficult," he fumbled to explain. "Nothing in life made sense." Time passed in a blur. Months flew by. Holidays were ignored. "Since I began working at the station, I've been more alive the past couple of months than I have the past six years." He brushed a strand of hair from her cheek. "And you, Anastazia Nowakowski, are the reason."

The blond Polish bombshell had knocked his world off kilter. For good or bad? Too soon to tell. "I wish I could hide the scars, Anna. They're repulsive." If only he could erase the image of her shocked reaction from his memory. "The surgeon had to remove part of the muscle from my shoulder." He remembered the agonizing physical-therapy sessions he'd suffered through to regain eighty percent of the movement in his left arm—thirty percent more than doctors had predicted.

Anna sniffed. "I was appalled by the sight, but not

for the reasons you imagine." She laid her cold fingers against his cheek. Her gaze, warm and tender, urged Ryan to rest his head against hers and soak up all the care and concern she possessed for him.

"My first thought," she continued, "was, dear God, the pain you must have suffered."

"I wish I could admit that I was brave, and courageous, and fought the good fight." But he hadn't. He trained his gaze on the ocean. "In the beginning, I wasn't aware of the extent of my injuries. One afternoon my wife walked into the room while the nurses were cleaning my wounds. Her face…" He couldn't make himself describe the repulsive twist of his wife's mouth or the sound of her retching in the hall outside his room.

"That evening Sandra apologized, but she couldn't even make eye contact with me. I believed our relationship wouldn't survive in the long run. Why drag out the inevitable? So I asked for a divorce. To Sandra's credit, she made a halfhearted attempt to talk me into a separation. She was worried about how others would view her if we divorced so soon after I'd been injured. I was doped up and in a lot of pain and I said some terrible things to her. Called her names. Accused her of inexcusable things."

"But you loved each other, didn't you?"

"Yes. But our marriage had been strained even before 9/11. Sandra had hoped to start a family. I kept putting her off. I was traveling a lot and working long hours." He took a steadying breath. "That's what made my behavior unforgivable."

When he didn't explain, Anna encouraged him. "Finish the story, Ryan. Tell me everything."

"The day after our argument, Sandra miscarried. She

hadn't even realized she'd been pregnant. I blamed myself. If I hadn't called her those awful names...if I hadn't upset her..."

"The miscarriage wasn't your fault or Sandra's. Those things just happen."

"I hadn't believed I wanted a baby, but the news that we'd lost a child showed me otherwise."

"Shh..." Anna wrapped her arms around him.

"I'm to blame for my child not living." He hugged her fiercely. Buried his face in her neck. "After hearing we'd lost a baby, I gave up on everything, including me."

"I'm glad you are who you are, Ryan, or I never would have had this moment with you." She found his mouth and her kiss conveyed how badly she desired him—damaged goods and all.

"Let's go back to the room. We'll search for Parnell later."

Without speaking a word, she stood and offered her hand. He couldn't predict what the future held for them, but Anna's unconditional acceptance lent him the courage to move one step closer to her.

"Ryan? Are you all right?" Anna's muted voice drifted beneath the bathroom door.

Fully clothed, Ryan sat on the toilet lid, counting the squares in the black-and-white tiled floor. He'd returned to the hotel room a half hour ago, eagerly anticipating making love. He suspected Anna had slipped into a slinky nightgown. Despite his agony, he smiled. *No.* Anna would prefer a Giants football jersey.

He had to answer her. But how? Anna, would you mind if I leave my clothes on, just unzip my pants and... He'd been positive he could do this—get naked with a woman. But Anna wasn't any woman. Anna was…Anna. She'd reached deep inside him to the place he believed he'd sealed off forever. She'd wiggled through his defenses, and now here he was…about to lay more than his soul bare.

"May I come in?" The quiet plea squeezed his heart.

For the past few minutes he'd listened to the patter of her feet as she paced the hallway. Why was this so difficult? Shoving a hand through his hair, he answered, "Door's open."

Anna poked her head around the edge. When she noticed he hadn't undressed, her blue eyes softened. "Everything okay?"

The concern in her voice clawed at his heart, leaving him with his throat swollen and unable to answer. He shrugged, angry and embarrassed he couldn't get a handle on his emotions.

She slipped into the room, shut the door and leaned against it. The corners of his mouth curved when he noticed her full attire—a Giants football jersey. She plucked at the helmet logo plastered across the front of the material. "I'm not really a Victoria's Secret kind of girl." Her gaze passed over his face, then glued itself to the floor.

Her pink toenails winked beneath the fluorescent lights. He noticed how sturdy and wide her feet were. Strong feet. Strong enough, he wondered, to hold him up through this experience?

Agitated, he went to the sink and gripped the sides of the porcelain bowl. He'd attempted sex once after his divorce. The lights had been out, the woman had been drunk and he'd kept his shirt on. But the demons had escaped, and he'd panicked and fled before anything had happened.

Head bent, eyes closed, he confessed, "I didn't expect it to be this difficult." Damn, he was stumbling badly. "It has nothing to do with you." *Liar. It has everything to do with Anna.* She possessed the power to convince him to forgive himself and get on with his life. What if he disappointed her?

Caring hands rubbed his back, then slid around his middle. She rested her cheek against his damaged shoulder. Those lush breasts caused a certain part of his anatomy to stir. His body craved sex. His heart wanted unconditional acceptance.

Her careful strokes lulled him into a state of lethargy. Not until he heard the scrape of her long nails against his skin did he realize she'd snuck her hands beneath his shirt. Her caresses left a path of goose pimples across his torso. When she tweaked his nipples, he groaned, the sound rumbling through his chest. Her fingers danced to the waistband of his trousers. Flirted with the hairs on his belly. He sucked in his stomach and held his breath. Waiting… Wanting…

When he opened his eyes, he discovered Anna watching him in the mirror. Blue eyes spoke to brown eyes…. *Let me heal you.*

I don't want you to be repulsed.

There's nothing repulsive about you.

If you change your mind, you can stop.

I won't change my mind. Let me love you, Ryan.

On tiptoe, she kissed his neck, then her clever fingers bunched the hem of his shirt and shoved the material up his chest. When she could go no farther, her eyes sought his in the mirror.

I can do this. For Anna. He lifted his arms and she whisked the shirt over his head.

Wonder spread over her face as she caressed his puckered, grotesque flesh. Then she pressed her mouth to the deformed muscle. Heaven help him. He closed his eyes and fought to control his emotions before they overpowered him and he crumbled at her feet.

He focused on his body's physical reaction, rejoicing in the rush of adrenaline that pumped through his muscles, reassuring him that his male plumbing worked fine.

Showing no mercy, Anna slid her magical hands inside his briefs and cupped him. Stroked him. Held him. He lowered his head and groaned. Her tongue dipped inside his ear and he jerked. Her giggle eased his tension and he relaxed, leaning more fully against her, allowing her greater access to his loins. Taking advantage of the position, she explored the length of him. Her lips nibbled his neck, his face, his shoulder. But not where he needed them most.

He spun her, grabbed her by the shoulders and backed her up against the door. He wanted her mouth. Open. Wide. Lots of tongue. While he devoured her lips, her fingers tore at his belt, lowered his zipper, pushed his pants out of the way, taking the briefs with them. He shoved her nightshirt up to her waist, relieved to discover she wasn't wearing panties. He played with the moist curls between her thighs, until she was as ready for him as he was for her. Then he lifted her thigh and rested it over his hip. Foreplay was over. In one smooth thrust he entered her.

"I can't, I can't…" he muttered, pounding into her. He cupped her head to protect it from bumping the door. It ended before it had even begun, his release so shattering he cried out in shock and awe. Anna held him, cradled him, protected him. Exhausted, he rested his head in the crook of her neck, amazed that she was strong enough to hold him up.

They stood tangled together against the door for a long time before he slipped from her body. He reversed their positions and held her close, nuzzling his face in her hair. He prayed he wouldn't lose it in front of her. His chest threatened to explode from raw emotion. "I'm sorry, honey." His voice cracked and he cursed his weakness. "It's been so long…I couldn't—"

"You don't hear me complaining, do you?"

Tears pricked his eyes. What had he done to deserve this woman? This moment of joy?

Wrapped around each other, they stood until Ryan's body cooled and his sanity surfaced. "Sweet Jesus, Anna." He tilted her chin and gazed into her eyes. "I didn't use a condom." The box of protection was in the bedroom.

"I'll be fine. I'm at the beginning of my cycle. And in case you're wondering, I don't have any communicable diseases."

"Me, either."

Anna grinned and Ryan returned her smile. "What's so funny?"

"Discussing sexually transmitted diseases isn't very romantic."

"Neither is conversing with your pants around your ankles." He kissed her well-loved mouth. "What do you say we move this party to the bedroom?"

"Thought you'd never ask." She jumped into his arms and Ryan stumbled sideways, almost landing them in the tub. Chuckling at her playfulness, he worked his feet free of his pants and briefs. Naked save for black dress socks, he carried Anna through the suite and dropped her in the middle of the bed. He stretched out next to her, then worked the jersey up over her head and tossed the material to the floor.

Anna held her breath while Ryan studied her. The two men she'd slept with in the past had both been put off by her large breasts and hadn't paid much attention to them. She really wanted Ryan to appreciate all of her, big boobs, curvy thighs and more than a handful in the derriere department.

The awe on his face eased her fears. He pushed her breasts together, then buried his face between them. "Every inch of you is gorgeous, Anna."

That Ryan appreciated her physique helped Anna relax and enjoy his erotic touches and hot, intimate kisses.

"Mmm," he groaned against her nipple. "My turn to play." His hands and mouth were everywhere at once, building sensation on top of sensation. He delighted in making her squirm and…beg.

Desperate for relief from the escalating tension winding through her, she butted his shoulders until he offered her his attention. "I need you," she whispered. Pressing her hand against the back of his head, she brought his mouth to hers and kissed him with every ounce of feeling she possessed. She drew her legs up and dug her heels into the mattress. Open. Exposed. Vulnerable.

A condom materialized from the nightstand drawer and he sheathed himself. Mouths fused, he slid home. The relief Anna sought never came. Stroke after stroke after stroke, the pressure continued to build. Her hips thrashed, but Ryan's hands steadied her. He drove Anna to the edge, where she hovered, waiting for him to shove her over and free her soul.

Instead of freeing her, Ryan drew out her agony by

flipping their positions. Now Anna straddled him. Pushed beyond her limit, she rode him with wild abandon. He added to her torment when he leaned forward and lavished attention on her breasts as his hand snaked between her thighs. One, two, three caresses and Anna went soaring off the cliff.

Head swinging from side to side, her long hair dusting the tops of Ryan's thighs, she moaned her release. Caught up in her own climax, she barely heard Ryan's masculine shout. She collapsed on his chest, her cheek stuck to his slick skin. Never had she been this emotionally, this physically drained. Tears dribbled down her face and plopped onto his shoulder. With the pad of her thumb, she smeared the wetness across the scarred flesh.

"Tears?" A worry line formed between his eyebrows.

"Nothing's wrong. Everything's right," she insisted. For the first time in her life, Anastazia Nowakowski had offered her whole heart to someone—Ryan.

Ryan kissed her. A slow, thorough caress. No words. No promises. Only a kiss.

For now, that was enough.

ANNA SNUGGLED deeper into Ryan's arms, reveling in his warm, solid body. She imagined waking each morning next to him. Sharing a smile. A kiss. She'd learned more about him in the past twenty-four hours than she had the past couple of months—except for one thing. Why had he signed on with Parnell Brothers?

"Spit it out," Ryan grumbled.

"Spit what out?" She'd assumed he'd been asleep.

"Whatever's troubling you. Your sighs are driving me crazy."

Okay. He asked for it. "Why are you working at the rubbish company? It's obvious you don't need the money." She held her breath, hoping the question hadn't ruined their newfound intimacy. Seconds elapsed into a lengthy silence. One by one, his muscles hardened to rock.

Her first instinct was to say, *Never mind.* But she stopped herself. This was important. Ryan was important. She wasn't positive when or how it had happened, but suddenly she wasn't willing to settle for a make-believe family the rest of her life. No more portraits of strangers. No more pretending her coworkers were distant relatives. She yearned for her very own *real* family. Loving Ryan made her realize that living on the fringes of other people's lives wasn't enough. She deserved more—a husband and another child, one she could be a real mother to.

"Hungry?" he asked.

So much for an answer. Maybe now wasn't the time to push him. Besides, she had secrets, too. "I guess I could eat."

"We skipped lunch and went straight to dessert." He scooted lower in the bed and kissed her neck. Ah, he made it easy to let him off the hook. The nuzzling stopped and his face hovered above hers, his expression serious. "What happened to your mother?" he asked.

Men. She supposed he expected an answer, even when he'd avoided her question a few moments ago. *Maybe if you open up first, Ryan will follow.* His question hadn't surprised her. People were naturally curious to learn how she'd ended up in foster care. "My mother died of alcohol poisoning. A guest alerted the motel manager to a nasty odor in one of the rooms. She'd been dead a week when the police found her."

"Jesus, Anna. Where were you all that time?"

"I was four years old and don't remember much. The information in my case file says I was a passenger on a bus destined for Kansas City."

"Alone?" Outrage flashed in his eyes.

"Not at first." After all these years, Anna still hurt that her mother had put her in such danger. "We boarded at the Port Authority. When we stopped in Cleveland, my mother left me. I must have fallen asleep, because another passenger alerted the bus driver before he drove too far that I'd been abandoned."

"You could have been kidnapped or molested," Ryan declared.

Or killed. "The police were contacted. Social services picked me up at the next stop and I was brought back to New York City. The authorities searched for my mother in Cleveland, but she'd already returned to New York." Again tears leaked from Anna's eyes and she sniffed.

Ryan brushed the wetness from her cheeks. "What happened next, honey?"

"They put me in a temporary foster home. When my mother turned up dead, they looked for relatives."

"Oh, baby." He kissed her temple. "Such a brave girl."

She had been brave, hadn't she?

"Did they locate any relatives?"

"A grandmother and an aunt. Neither had the resources to care for me. By the time I entered high school, my grandmother had passed away and my aunt had moved from the city. Not that it mattered. They never had any contact with me."

"She left you on a bus…." Ryan shook his head in disgust. "I can't imagine any woman willingly giving up her child."

Anna's heart beat erratically for several seconds. She thought of Tina, the tiny baby she'd offered up for adoption. She yearned to tell Ryan about her daughter. To share her memories of holding Tina for the first time and the sorrow of handing her to a stranger to raise.

"Hell of a Hallmark story, Nowakowski." Ryan rolled her beneath him and distracted her with kisses and caresses.

She threw herself into the moment. Allowed herself to enjoy, to savor the here and now with Ryan. Because deep in her heart she believed this Little Orphan Anna's tale was destined for an unhappy ending.

Chapter Eleven

"You have mustard…" Anna pointed at the corner of Ryan's mouth as they strolled along the Boardwalk, eating corn dogs.

"Where?" He stopped, lowered his head and wiggled his eyebrows suggestively, daring her to remove the mustard smudge—not with her thumb but her…

Oh, yeah. Her tongue flicked his skin. Not once but three times before sneaking inside his mouth. Now who was teasing whom?

"Mmm… I believe I could kiss you forever, Ryan Jones," she muttered before stepping away.

At her mention of his alias, the half-eaten corn dog churned in his stomach. He should have come clean with her after they'd made love. Anna deserved at least that from him. Rather than ruin the moment with such a confession, he stood in the chilly sunshine and absorbed her sweet, crooked-tooth smile and sparkling blue eyes. He laid a cold palm against her cheek and gazed at her face, trying to say without words how much he cared for her.

Love. Was that the name of the soulful yearning stirring in his chest? He'd gladly admit to caring deeply for Anna. Her Pollyanna attitude had lifted him from the dark and carried him to the light, coaxing him to engage in life. But love—the forever kind?

Sandra's image popped into his mind. He wished he could blame his ex-wife for being the one to quit on him, but he couldn't. He'd been the one to give up. The one afraid their relationship wouldn't survive after 9/11. In self-defense he'd left her before she had the opportunity to leave him. He'd destroyed Sandra, himself, their marriage and their unborn child.

Had he learned his lesson with Sandra? Could he promise Anna he'd never inflict the pain on her that he'd caused his first wife? He had no control over the future. Nor could he control a possible catastrophic event that might test their... What—*love?* Maybe he shouldn't allow things between them to become serious. Oh, hell. His feelings were already serious.

"What's wrong, Ryan?" Anna's brow wrinkled. Perhaps their lovemaking had increased her ability to read his mind or he had lost the capacity to hide his emotions from her. A bit of both, he assumed.

"Nothing's wrong." He kissed the tip of her red nose. "I'm wondering where to search for Parnell."

Anna nibbled the last bit of corn dog, then threw the stick into the garbage can behind Ryan. Her gaze skimmed his face before attaching itself to an empty bench farther up the Boardwalk. "I feel guilty," she blurted. "We came here to find Bobby and—" she looked him straight in the eye "—all I want to do is return to the room and make love again." Two bright red blotches stained her cheeks.

Tucking her against his side, he whispered, "Thank you."

"For what?"

"For caring about me." *For making me feel like a man again.* "I'm glad we had today."

"Me, too."

He wanted to promise her there'd be more opportunities for lovemaking tomorrow, the next day or even the next month. But he wouldn't make a pledge he wasn't certain he could keep.

"Your pants are ringing." Anna grinned.

"Maybe this is James." Ryan had asked the Trump Plaza manager to advise the other hotel managers along the Boardwalk to keep an eye out for Parnell.

After a brief exchange with James, Ryan snapped the phone shut. "Parnell's here."

"Where?" Anna clutched his coat sleeve.

"The Tropicana. He's playing blackjack." Taking her hand, they changed course. "He's been at the table since late last night." When they entered the Tropicana, Ryan instructed, "Wait here, Anna."

"But—"

"Let me coax Parnell away from the table and bring him to the lobby. He might become distressed when he sees you." No telling what shape the man was in or how much he'd drunk.

"Be patient with him," Anna called out as he walked away.

Patient? He supposed he could be charitable, since he and Anna would never have had this time together if Parnell hadn't snuck off to Atlantic City.

Spotting their boss didn't take long—he was sitting alone at a table. In his rush to get to Atlantic City, Parnell must have forgotten his razor. A full beard covered his face and he wore a rumpled church suit and stained tie. Ryan stopped next to him and winced as he caught a whiff of unwashed body and booze. He signaled to the dealer to leave them.

"Hey, I'm not finished," Parnell called out.

"Time to go, boss." Ryan thumped Parnell's shoulder.

"Jones?" Parnell glanced around Ryan, no doubt checking to see if the rest of the guys at the station had tagged along. "What are you doing here?" he grumbled.

"Saving your ass." He grabbed a fistful of Parnell's suit jacket and coaxed him off the chair. "Anna's not going to appreciate your being in such a sorry state," Ryan muttered.

Parnell dug in his heels. "Anna's here?"

• "She's worried about you."

"I...I... No." He shook his head. "I don't want—"

"You should have thought of that before you embarked on another one of your gambling binges." He tugged and Parnell followed. "A pot of coffee and a shower will do you more good than another hand of blackjack," Ryan muttered.

The moment Anna spotted them, she rushed forward and flung her arms around her boss. Ryan resisted the urge to punch Parnell for causing her grief.

"Mary's worried. We're all concerned about you." Anna brushed at the wrinkles in his jacket.

Shamefaced, Parnell dropped his gaze to the floor. "Things are—"

"Let's go." Ryan ushered them out of the hotel. No need to air Parnell's dirty laundry in the Tropicana lobby. "Where are you staying?" he asked when they stepped outside.

Parnell offered a blank look.

"Bobby." Anna pulled on his coat sleeve. "Where's your hotel room?"

"I don't have one," he mumbled.

That explained his smell. Ryan steered him toward the sidewalk. "When did you arrive in Atlantic City?"

"What's today?" Parnell asked.

"Saturday," Anna said.

"Then I got here Wednesday night."

Anna frowned. "Where have you slept?"

Bloodshot eyes pleaded with Ryan. Taking pity on the man, he insisted, "We'll talk when we get to the hotel." He and Anna flanked the boss as they walked to the Trump Plaza. They stopped once to buy Parnell coffee from a street vendor.

By the time they arrived in the hotel room, Anna's mothering had caught up to speed and she hovered over Parnell, urging him to eat, then changing her mind and telling him to sleep, then suggesting he might want to shower first.

The man didn't deserve Anna's attention. Irritated, Ryan pulled her aside, shoved two hundred dollars in her hand and suggested she purchase a change of clothes for the boss from one of the hotel boutiques. While she shopped, he intended to help Parnell shower and shave. "Let him recover his dignity before we grill him with questions," he whispered.

"I'll reimburse you for whatever I spend."

"Don't worry about the money," he insisted.

"You're certain you can…" She nodded to Parnell, who slouched on the sofa.

"Give us an hour."

"Fine." Instead of heading to the door, she went up on tiptoe and kissed him. "Thank you for caring. For…everything."

Ryan didn't miss the emphasis placed on *everything*.

She pressed her mouth to his again—not a sweet peck, but an I-want-you kiss—then she strolled out the door.

"It's that way between the two of you, huh?"

"My relationship with Anna isn't any of your business." Ryan faced Parnell. "Besides, you're in no shape to protest."

He snorted, spit spraying from his mouth. "But my gambling is your business?"

"Anything that impacts Anna concerns me."

Parnell's mouth thinned, but he held his tongue and slumped into a ball of defeat, the fight drained out of him.

"Is this a short-lived gambling binge or are you in real trouble?"

Parnell rallied. "What makes you believe I'm in trouble?"

"Anna discovered money missing from the company accounts. And she's aware of your previous gambling problem."

"She's too damn nosy for her own good."

"Nosy or not, Anna cares about you and your wife and wants to help. I'm not sure you deserve help." Before the man went off on a tangent, Ryan demanded, "Answer my question. Are you in trouble?"

After a pregnant pause, Parnell confessed, "Big trouble."

"How much are you in for?"

"I'm gonna lose the business."

"What?" Ryan shot out of the chair. Parnell dived for cover behind the couch. This was worse than Ryan had imagined. "Are you talking bankruptcy?"

White-knuckling the sofa cushions, Parnell whined, "I got in too deep with a loan shark."

"Loan shark? Are you talking the mob?"

"I owe Little Nicky over three hundred thousand dollars."

"Who the hell is Little Nicky?"

"You haven't heard of Little Nicky?" The awe in Parnell's voice was almost comical.

Manhattan might as well be a continent away from Queens, because Ryan had no idea who the mobster was. "I've never heard of the man."

"Godfather Scarlotto. You've heard of the Scarlotto brothers, haven't you?"

Unable to remember if he had or hadn't heard the mob name, Ryan shrugged.

"Little Nicky floated me a loan. I was winning a month ago, but I hit a rough patch and…" The boss sucked in a noisy breath. "Then Mary left me and I…I couldn't stop rolling the dice. I kept thinking that if I won a lot of money, Mary would take me back." Parnell gnawed the tips of his nails and Ryan winced at the sight of a once-strong man now lost and insecure. He almost felt sorry for the guy. Almost.

"What happens if you can't pay this jerk?"

"Little Nicky's not so bad."

"He's a mobster!" Lack of sleep and food deprivation must have numbed Parnell's brain cells.

"You're thinking of the movie *The Godfather*. Times have changed. The mob doesn't go around shooting people who can't pay their debts."

"How do they collect their money?"

"By seizing personal property."

"The station."

Parnell nodded.

"If you paid off Little Nicky, you'd be able to keep the business?"

"No. I signed over the business in exchange for a hundred thousand cash."

"Tell me you're joking." Parnell wasn't that stupid. "You owe this guy over 300K, and even if you find the money to pay him, he keeps Parnell Brothers."

"Yeah."

"What the hell was going through your mind? You can't screw with people's lives. Anna and the others need their jobs."

"I *wasn't* thinking, okay!" He smacked a couch pillow, sending it flying across the room.

Anger burned in Ryan's gut. Parnell Brothers was all Anna had. Losing her job and the connection with the other men would destroy her. "How long before Anna and the others are unemployed?"

"First week in November."

Only a few days to figure out a solution to the quagmire. "C'mon. You could use a shower."

Shoulders sagging, Parnell shuffled to the bathroom.

"Don't say a word to Anna or anyone else until I—"

"You could ask your grandfather if he'd bail me out," Parnell interrupted.

Ryan stopped in the hallway. "My grandfather? What does he have to do with this?"

"He paid off my previous debt to Little Nicky on the condition that I offer you a job."

"My grandfather has connections with the mob?"

"You mean you didn't know?"

"GRANDPA, it's me, Ryan."

"Ryan, my boy. Good to hear from you. Everything okay?"

Not really. Ryan rested on the end of the hotel bed

while Parnell showered and shaved. He expected Anna to return with clothes for the boss any minute, so he planned to make the call short—which meant cutting to the chase and dispensing with pleasantries. "Are you involved with the mob?"

The soft whir of the connection greeted Ryan's ears. His grandfather's silence signified guilt. "Your name and Little Nicky's came up in the same conversation."

"I have no idea what you're talking about, young man. I have never done anything illegal—"

"Grandpa, Parnell confessed you paid off a debt he owed the mob in order to land a job for me."

"Parnell has a leaky mouth," the old man grumbled.

"Yeah, well, the man's got leaky pockets, too. He's in more hot water with the mob."

"I'm listening."

At the hint of exhaustion in his grandfather's voice, Ryan suffered a twinge of remorse. For thirty-five years, Patrick McKade had been a pillar of strength for him and his brothers, a man who'd supported them in good and in bad times. "Look, Grandpa—"

"Don't you *look* me, grandson. What's going on? Between the two of us, we'll figure out a solution."

"Parnell went on a gambling binge again. Little Nicky's seizing the business."

"How much is he in for?"

"Over three hundred thousand. He claims he signed over the station for a hundred thousand."

"Have the station appraised and see what its worth is."

Once in a while his grandfather's thoughts jumped so far ahead, trying to keep pace was similar to peddling a bike after the chain fell off. "Why?"

"I had assumed you wanted to purchase the company from the mob."

Now that his grandfather had voiced the idea... "I could make an offer." For a guy who preferred to live in isolation, he was throwing himself in the fire on this one—but he'd do anything to help Anna and the others keep their jobs.

"Buying the business won't solve the problem in the long run," his grandfather contested.

"What do you mean?"

"Once a gambler, always a gambler. How will you prevent Parnell from putting the business up a second time in exchange for another loan from the mob?"

"Easy. McKade Import-Export will hold the legal rights to the business and I propose that Anna run the show. Parnell can keep his name on the station and continue working in some capacity if he cares to, but he won't have access to the company's finances."

"Who do you have in mind for that responsibility— you?"

Ryan contemplated a change of career for all of two seconds. "As much as I haven't minded working with my hands, I prefer building the McKade bank accounts to cleaning them out. I trust Anastazia Nowakowski to safeguard the company's earnings."

"Ah. The Polish girl."

"How did you learn she was Polish?"

"With Nowakowski for a name? Does she have a good head for numbers?"

"She's been acting boss for a while now. More important, she's loyal." Ryan considered the way Anna put the needs of others before herself. "She'll do everything in her power to keep the company afloat."

"Sounds as if you admire this woman."

"I do." He understood his grandfather wished to see all his grandsons married off with families of their own before he died. He wanted to inform his grandfather that he'd found happy-ever-after with Anna, but he couldn't. Not until he knew where he stood with her. "We're just friends." *And a whole lot more.*

"You've got a few more weeks left on the job. Anything can happen."

He and Anna *had* happened. He thought of how far he'd stepped out of his shell since he'd arrived at Parnell Brothers. "I realize I fought you in the beginning, Grandpa, but…thank you. For forcing me to accept this job. Forcing me to admit that I have a lot of living left to do."

"I've always been proud of you, Ryan. It was simply a matter of time before you found your way back."

"Well, I'm back, old man."

His grandfather chortled with glee. "These life lessons for you and your brothers have cost me too much money. Next time I'll just swat all your arses."

"I love you." Ryan's throat tightened. He couldn't remember ever telling the old man that he loved him.

"You be careful dealing with Little Nicky. You don't want that handsome face of yours rearranged."

"Bye, Grandpa."

Ryan hung up the phone and pondered how to outcon a con man into helping him keep Anna's family together.

AFTER RUNNING an errand to the hardware store for Leon, Ryan parked his coworker's truck along the railroad tracks across the street from Mo's Tavern, then cut the engine. He studied the seedy bar, which at ten-thirty in the morning was deserted, even though an Open sign hung in the front window. Ryan checked the address on the piece of paper Parnell had given him. Yep. This was the Scarlotto family headquarters.

Eager to get the visit over with, Ryan left the truck, hustled across the street and entered the bar. He paused inside the door while his eyes adjusted to the dim interior.

"You wanna drink or what?" the oily-headed bartender inquired, a cigarette butt dangling from his mouth. A halo of smoke circled the man's head—but there was nothing angelic about him. A gruesome scar dissected one side of his face, beginning at the outer edge of his left eye, traveling across his cheek, then curving in and splitting his lower lip in half. Obviously, the guy had found himself on the wrong end of a knife blade.

"I'm here to see Nicky."

Ryan caught the almost imperceptible pause of the dishrag swish-swashing across the bar. "Nicky expecting you?" The nasally voice must have resulted from the guy having had his nose smashed in a few times.

"Figured I'd drop in." Before the barkeep hollered for Bruno the Bouncer to escort him from the premises, Ryan added, "My business concerns Parnell Brothers."

"Wait here."

The man disappeared through a door at the back. Ryan cozied up to the bar. Getting ready for work this morning had been more difficult than he'd expected. He wasn't physically tired, but the weekend in Atlantic City had emotionally exhausted him and hadn't ended the way he'd hoped—in Anna's bed.

After Anna had purchased clothes for Parnell, Ryan had decided they drive back to Queens that night. He hadn't trusted himself to keep his hands off Anna if they'd stayed at the hotel. And he hadn't wanted to get naked with her while Parnell snoozed on the couch in the living room. That Anna had been disappointed in ending their weekend early had soothed his male ego.

The trip to Queens had been made in silence. Parnell had slept in the backseat and Anna had dozed in the front, allowing him plenty of time for his brain to stew. He'd mentally replayed his and Anna's lovemaking, until he'd almost run the car off the pavement making a tight turn. After the near disaster, he'd forced himself to focus on the station's precarious situation.

When they'd parked at Parnell's friend's house, Anna had reassured Bobby that everything would be fine and she'd manage the business until he got back on his feet again. Hell, Anna had been running Parnell Brothers on and off for months.

Later that night alone in his sterile apartment, Ryan decided he was no better than Parnell. He, too, had quit on life, except he preferred to call it surviving. But after making love with Anna, *surviving* no longer appeared to be a great game plan.

"Little Nicky'll see you now," the bartender announced, stepping out of the shadows.

With a nod of thanks, Ryan approached the open door at the end of the hall. Godfather Scarlotto was six feet five inches, with the build of a California redwood. No wonder Parnell had acted nervous when they'd discussed the mobster. Little Nicky pointed his cigar to the chair in front of the desk.

Ryan sat.

"Slick says you got business with Parnell Brothers."

Slick. Fitting name for a man who appeared to wear the entire contents of a bottle of baby oil on his head. "I'm working temporarily for Parnell."

Eyes narrowing, Nicky grunted, "Don't bother me none who you work for."

"I understand he's into you for a lot of money."

"He can keep my money. I'll keep his business."

"What if Parnell raises the cash plus interest on what he owes you?"

Fleshy lips curved upward. "I charge a hundred and fifty percent interest."

"As I said, what if Parnell is good for the money?"

Dark, beady eyes glared. The *tick tock* of a wall clock echoed about the room. After a full minute Ryan swore his heart beat the same rhythm.

"Who the hell are you again?"

"McKade. Ryan McKade. You might recall doing business with my grandfather, Patrick McKade."

A beefy hand slapped the top of the desk and Ryan jumped inside his skin. The big ox had lightning reflexes. "Your grandfather paid off Parnell's debts."

"Name your price." Ryan suspected any man with money was a good man in Little Nicky's opinion.

"I don't want your money. I want Parnell's business."

Time to find out if a mob man had a heart or at least half a heart. "Good people are going to lose their jobs. They've got elderly parents to care for and children to—"

"Let them find other jobs."

So much for the heart angle. He had to protect Anna and the others. Anna more than anyone would be devastated if the station closed. She'd lose everything important to her. *Except you. She could have you…if you'd let her.* "Why a rubbish-removal company?"

Meaty fingers tapped the desktop. The mobster wasn't accustomed to explaining his actions. "I'll ask the questions," he growled. "What's a McKade doing poking around in trash?"

Hadn't he read somewhere that mob families had great respect for their elders? Ryan opted for the truth. "My grandfather believed I needed to be taught a lesson."

"What kind of lesson?"

"Bravery."

A lengthy silence ensued as the mobster ogled the wall behind Ryan. Finally, he inquired, "What are you afraid of?"

"Living." Ryan cringed. The truth was painful. "I was badly burned during the 9/11 attack. A few weeks later, I had a terrible fight with my wife. Not long after, she miscarried our baby and we divorced."

Sympathy darkened Little Nicky's eyes to black—or maybe it was a trick of the light reflecting off the dusky patches of skin above his cheekbones.

"I coped by shutting out the world. My grandfather accused me of being afraid of life and sentenced me to a blue-collar job where I'd be forced to interact with people."

Gaze boring into Ryan, Little Nicky confessed, "My uncle died in the first tower."

"I'm sorry." Multiply the sentiment by the thousands for every man, woman and child affected directly or indirectly by the terrorist attack.

"Why do you care if I take Parnell's business?"

"I respect the employees. They're hardworking people who want to provide the best for their families."

"Paying off Parnell's debt won't stop him from gambling again."

"You could refuse him when he asks for another loan," Ryan suggested.

"He deals with me because I treat him fair and his roots go deep in the community. I don't use a baseball bat to resolve disputes. If I send him away, he'll find another bookie who may not be as well mannered." The man grinned, showing off a gold eyetooth.

"What does the mob want with a garbage company?"

"If I told you, McKade, I'd have to kill you." Little Nicky chortled at the lame joke.

"Parnell has people who are concerned about him. People who will guarantee he receives help for his gambling addiction."

"Good for him." The mob boss checked his watch. "We're finished." He stood.

"Will you at least consider allowing Parnell to keep the business if he pays the money he owes?"

"No." Flat. Cold. Final.

"Would you consider—"

"Tell Parnell he has until November 5. Now, scat, rich boy."

"This isn't over," Ryan threatened.

"Perhaps your grandfather got your lesson wrong?"

"How's that?"

Respect shone in Little Nicky's eyes. "It took balls to come here."

"Yeah, well, you haven't seen the last of my balls." Ryan exited the room before he got real ballsy and told the mob boss to shove his loan where the daylight didn't shine.

Chapter Twelve

Following his nonproductive meeting with Little Nicky, Ryan had gone back to the job site—a cleanout on the west side of Queens. He'd brushed off Leon's complaint that he'd spent too long to purchase a sledgehammer at the hardware store.

The sledgehammer had come in handy, as Ryan used an interior wall to purge his anger at Parnell and his gambling obsession. In record time, he'd crushed the partition separating the living room from the kitchen, leaving Leon and Eryk gaping.

Now, after eight hours, Ryan was sore, tired and eager to see Anna. Leon guided the truck into the station garage. The second dump truck rested in its bay. While his coworkers went to collect their lunch boxes, Ryan went in search of Anna, who never left the office until all the guys checked in at the end of the day.

Ryan missed Anna. Missed her touch. Her scent. Her sweetness.

After they'd made love in Atlantic City, he'd selfishly hoped Parnell wouldn't surface so he and Anna could spend every hour, minute, second of the weekend together. She'd awoken in him a deep need to connect with another human being. A need he'd sworn had shriveled up and died after his divorce.

That *need* had eaten at him all week, until he believed he'd go crazy if he didn't spend some time with Anna—even a quick dinner before catching the train to Manhattan later that night.

The front office was empty, Anna's desk neat and tidy. Her coat was absent from the stand in the corner, and the coffeepot had been switched off. Frustrated, he entered the break room. "I guess Anna left early."

Eryk tapped the pink sticky note on the front of the fridge. *Have a headache. Went home early. See you tomorrow.*

Did Anna have a for-real headache, or… *Don't jump to conclusions.* They'd made love forty-eight hours ago. Too early to confirm if his one slipup had resulted in Anna becoming pregnant.

"You okay, Jones?" Eryk dropped into a chair at the table. "Sit before you pass out." He glanced at Leon. "He eat lunch?"

"Heard the flu's going around."

While Leon and Eryk exchanged flu stories, Ryan's heart bounced against his chest wall. The baby idea had materialized out of left field and had blindsided him. A second chance at fatherhood. The idea both excited and terrified him. Considering his screwed-up psyche, he'd probably make a mess of fatherhood.

Anna would guide you.

Part of Ryan ached to invest in the dream. But a child deserved two parents, and the thought of marriage—of trusting a person to stay by his side through good and bad—terrified him. He accepted the blame for his divorce. But in his defense, he'd reached out to Sandra after the news of her miscarriage. He'd made an attempt, albeit a feeble one. It had been too late. Ryan wondered if, with time, he could learn to trust Anna with his heart.

"You want a lift to the train, Jones? It's on my way," Leon offered.

"No, thanks. I've got an errand to run." Ryan intended to check on Anna.

"Flip the bottom lock on the side door when you leave," Leon instructed, then he and Eryk walked out.

Before closing up the station, Ryan grabbed a fast shower and changed into the extra set of clothes he'd stored in his locker. He caught the bus near the Muddy River Café and got off in Anna's neighborhood shortly thereafter. A brisk five-minute walk and he'd arrived at the brownstone apartment. He rang the bell, pressing his finger against the button longer than necessary.

"Chill!" a masculine voice called from inside.

The door swung open and Anna's roommate appeared, wearing a white apron and a chef's cap and wielding a wooden spoon covered with chocolate. The scowl on the guy's face evaporated and a curious gleam lit his eyes as his gaze roved Ryan from head to toe.

He was being checked out by another man and couldn't decide if the experience offended or amused him. "Is Anna here?"

"She's napping. I'm Blair, her roommate." He transferred the wooden spoon to his left hand and held out his right.

"Ryan Jones."

"Anna talks about you—" he rolled his eyes "—all the time. C'mon in." He waved the spoon and Ryan expected chocolate drops to splatter the walls, but the batter clung to the utensil. "I'm supposed to wake her in a few minutes."

Once inside the apartment, Ryan hovered near the door, resisting the urge to squirm under Blair's scrutiny. After the longest ten seconds of Ryan's life, Anna's roommate announced, "Keep me company while I finish my lesson." The man vanished into the kitchen.

Following the scent of baking chocolate, Ryan moved through the room, then hovered in the kitchen doorway. The place was a disaster. Pots, pans, dishes, measuring cups and spoons he'd never seen before littered the counters and tabletop. Amid the chaos, the oven timer bleeped.

"Ah, the first layer." Blair retrieved a pair of mitts in the shape of fish, then slid a pan from the oven and rested it on a wire rack to cool. "I'm experimenting with a recipe for my midterm exam." After inserting a toothpick into the middle of the cake, he touched, then sniffed, the splinter of wood. "Perfect," he announced.

Ryan was unsure what to say, but his stomach spoke for him. The rumbling echoed loud and clear in the tiny space.

"Sit down. You can be my guinea pig." Blair winked.

Never having been winked at by a man, Ryan chose to ignore the gesture. "If the cake tastes half as good as it smells, you ought to pass the test," he complimented Blair.

"I prepared the amaretto frosting last night." Blair fetched a ceramic bowl from the fridge. Next he cut a large piece of still-hot cake. He wielded the spatula as if the utensil were an artist's paintbrush. The end product was a masterpiece of delicate swirls and spikes.

Blair sat down opposite Ryan at the table, rested his chin in his palm and waited for a verdict. The cake, a unique combination of amaretto and chocolate, melted in Ryan's mouth. "Unbelievable."

Preening under the compliment, the chef flashed his even, white teeth. "My own creation."

"I don't cook, but I'd give this an A plus." Ryan didn't object when Blair placed a second, smaller piece in front of him, then added a glass of milk.

"Thanks."

"So." Blair tapped his fingertips on the tabletop. "Tell me about Ryan—the man who's responsible for Anna singing in the shower."

Ryan made it a policy to never discuss his women with other men.

"She never said, but I can tell." Blair leaned forward.

"Tell what?" Ryan was having difficulty following the discussion.

"Anna's in love with you. I think it's quite romantic, really."

Love? The forever kind, or the this-is-new-and-different kind? He believed her feelings were serious—she would have never slept with him if she didn't care deeply. But love? "I care very much for Anna," he admitted.

Blair sighed. *Again.* "I figured you were special when Anna's portrait family didn't scare you away."

"She's the one who's special. She's a survivor."

"Anna and I have been friends—" Blair paused, narrowing his gaze "—for a long time, so I'm entitled to ask. What are your intentions toward her?"

First Parnell and now Anna's roommate? Ryan wanted to insist his intentions were honorable, but a chance remained that he'd bail out in the end. "That's between Anna and me."

"You slept with her this past weekend," Blair accused.

"She told you?" Ryan hoped she'd left out at least

one detail—how they'd forgotten to use a condom the first time.

"Anna didn't say a word."

Resisting the urge to squirm in his seat, Ryan muttered, "I'm not in the habit of discussing my love life with—"

"Gay men?"

Scowling, Ryan finished his sentence. "With any-one." Then he added, "You have an annoying habit of interrupting people."

"You'll get used to it." Blair removed Ryan's empty dessert plate from the table and added it to the pile of dirty dishes stacked in the sink. "I have one more thing to say, then I'll drop the subject." His face sobered. "Don't break her heart."

"I'll do my best not to." He prayed his best was good enough.

"And in case the subject comes up…yes, I'm okay with you moving in with us."

Ryan had trouble picturing himself, Anna and Blair living together. On the other hand, Blair's cooking would be a bonus.

"Am I missing the party?" Anna rubbed her puffy eyes in the kitchen doorway.

The sight of her, all cuddly like a well-loved teddy bear, squeezed Ryan's heart. He rose from his chair, crossed the room and hugged her, not caring that they had an audience. Ryan loved how she curled into him when he rubbed her back. "Feeling better?"

"Lots better now that you're here."

Her words were a balm to his weary soul. Anna had a way of making him feel needed and desired. And scared. He worried about his deepening feelings for her, yet felt defenseless against the power she wielded over him. "Do you get headaches often?" He didn't dare ask if she was pregnant. Not with the roommate eavesdropping.

"Not very often. Blair made me his famous hangover remedy, then sent me to bed."

"I'm glad someone was here to look after you," Ryan said, ignoring the jealous twinge that caught him by surprise. He wished he'd been the one she'd turned to for help.

"How long have you been here?" she asked.

"Long enough to sample Blair's cake. Your roommate's a hell of a chef."

Once again, Blair preened under the compliment as he washed the mixing bowls in the sink.

"So the recipe worked?" Anna peeked around Ryan's shoulder.

"Better than I'd hoped. Sit and I'll cut you a piece," the resident chef invited.

"I will later. Right now I want to kiss Ryan." She snatched Ryan's hand and tugged him toward the hallway.

One of Blair's eyebrows lifted in an I-told-you-so gesture.

Shrugging, Ryan grinned, then allowed Anna to lead him to her bedroom at the end of the hallway. Once inside, she shut the door, rolled up on her tiptoes and kissed him.

For two seconds he hesitated, then he lifted her off the ground and walked her to the bed. They should talk, not make love. He suspected Blair could be right. Anna might be halfway in love with him already. And his feelings for her were traveling the same path. She deserved a commitment. At least a promise. But all he cared about at the moment was showing her how much he needed her. As if she were his next breath.

When the backs of her knees bumped the edge of the mattress, he collapsed with her in a heap on the bed. He paid particular attention to her mouth. "I wanted to kiss you as soon as I saw you at the station this morning," he mumbled, then trailed his lips over the silky column of her neck.

Anna's heated murmur fueled Ryan's desire and he worked his hands under her T-shirt, then fumbled with the front clasp on her bra until it popped open and her breasts spilled into his hands. Anna's sighs switched to earthy moans when he rubbed the pads of his thumbs across her rosy nipples. With her help, they worked the T-shirt over her head. Gathering her close, he feasted on her breasts, convinced he'd never tire of seeing, feeling, loving Anna's generous curves.

The way she arched her body, seeking his touch, warmed Ryan. He kissed her belly, nuzzling her tummy with his nose, while toying with the elastic band on her pink panties. Then he slid his fingers beneath the silk and caressed the soft blond curls at the juncture of her thighs.

A burst of sanity made him ask, "What about your roommate?"

"Blair won't bother us." She traced his mouth with the tip of her fingernail, and he had trouble focusing on her words. "Besides, he approves of you."

"I'm glad." Ryan swirled his tongue inside her belly button.

"He's never allowed any of my other dates to sample his cooking."

"Your roommate offered me a slice of cake because he approves of me?" Ryan nibbled her hip.

"And—" his hand slid inside her panties again and

she gasped "—because Blair trusts you." Grabbing a fistful of Ryan's hair, she tugged until he met her gaze. "I trust you, Ryan."

Trust—that funny, complicated, guilt-rendering five-letter word.

"What's wrong?" Blue eyes shimmered with anxiety. "Second thoughts?"

How about third? Fourth? He rubbed his mouth across hers. "I can't promise you anything except that this is where I want to be now. With you."

Cradling his face in her hands, Anna insisted, "And I want to be with you."

Her declaration confused more than comforted. If she cared deeply, why was she settling for this moment and not demanding the future? The coward in him yearned for her total commitment, her confession of love, without having to risk saying the words himself. Blocking out his subconscious, he focused on stripping her glorious body.

Clothes flew across the room; Ryan's shoes thudded against the rug. "Did you lock the door?" He peeled away her panties and tossed them over his shoulder.

"Blair won't barge in."

His aroused body beyond caring, Ryan shoved the beaded bed pillows to the floor, pulled back the red sateen comforter, then stretched out beside her. Anna's hands boldly explored his body, until Ryan was wild for her. When her talented hands brought him to the brink, he demanded, "My wallet, Anna. Find my wallet."

"Not to worry." She leaned over him, plastering her breasts to his chest, then made him squirm when her knee nudged his arousal. "I have a condom." She extracted one from the drawer in the bedside table and held it up for inspection. "Pink." With a sassy wink, she sheathed him. He gaped at the pink latex, praying his privates were color-blind.

Then Anna's mouth went to work and he wouldn't have protested if she had tied a bow around him. When she lowered herself onto him, her smile touched Ryan's heart and he shut his eyes against the surge of emotion. He was an idiot if he thought he could control his feelings for Anna. He more than cared for her. Damn it, he loved her!

Angry with himself for permitting her to slip past his defenses, he rolled her beneath him, shoved his tongue inside her mouth and pounded into her, desperately trying to exorcise his desire, his need for her.

If he was too rough, Anna didn't complain, which increased Ryan's desperation. Seconds from exploding, he came to his senses and slowed his pace.

"No, don't stop. Don't stop," Anna begged, wrapping her legs around his waist.

He didn't stop until he and Anna went off like a couple of Fourth of July fireworks.

Knock.

Ryan lifted one eyelid, his blurry vision cataloging his surroundings.

Knock.

His foggy brain connected the noise with the bedroom door.

Knock.

Instinct made him pull the sheet over his and Anna's naked bodies.

The door swung open and a grinning Blair entered with a tray of food. "Nourishment. Anna must eat to prevent another migraine." He delivered the tray to the nightstand near Ryan. Twin spots of red colored the man's cheeks when his gaze swept over Ryan's naked chest.

The last time Ryan had been caught naked with a female had been his senior year in college in the fraternity-house laundry room. "Thanks for the food."

"Make Anna eat before you go at it again." Blair paused at the door. "Tell her I have a date with Thatcher. If things go as planned, I'll be spending the night with him."

What the hell was Ryan supposed to say? "Ah, good luck, then."

"Thanks." Blair left, and once Ryan heard the front door slam, he sucked in a deep breath.

"He's happy for us," Anna murmured, her lips moving against Ryan's chest.

"He's so happy he had to barge in here with a tray of food?" He cuddled her and kissed the top of her head.

Anna giggled, and Ryan groaned at the sexy feel of her jiggling breasts against him. "He was checking to see if I was okay." She propped herself up against the headboard and played with Ryan's hair, twining the strands around her fingers. "You probably think our relationship is weird, but Blair's like a brother to me."

Shifting to his side, Ryan asked, "What's his story?"

After a lengthy pause, she inquired, "Do you really care or are you just curious?"

"I care about you, Anna." He stroked the pad of his thumb across her lower lip. "And Blair's important to you, so yeah, I care about him, too."

"His parents live on Long Island. When he confessed he was gay, they disowned him. Threw his clothes and personal things onto the front lawn, changed the locks on the door and got an unlisted telephone number."

"That's rough." On occasion Ryan or one of his brothers had failed their grandfather, but the geezer had never withheld his love from them.

"We met on a city bus. A drunk had been pestering me, and Blair stepped in and acted as my boyfriend so the jerk would go away. We ended up riding the same bus line and became friends. Then I mentioned I wished I could afford to rent one of the brownstone apartments on this street and he volunteered to be my roommate and share expenses. As here we are. Friends and roommates."

"He's lucky to have you, Anna." Ryan meant every word. He was relieved she had Blair to watch over her.

"I'm lucky to have you." Her kiss confirmed Ryan's greatest fear—Anna was in love with him. No, she hadn't said the words, but he suspected her love in the way she touched him, the way her lips played over his, the subtle looks she bequeathed him.

All these years he'd assumed he'd been empty inside. But Anna had discovered something worthwhile in him and had burrowed her way into his heart. If he could find the courage to try again with a woman, there was no doubt in his mind, that woman would be Anna. He hauled her close, shaken by how deeply she affected him. She filled his heart with gladness and warmth. And hope. He had Anna to thank for bringing him back to life…making him understand that he could go on.

His stomach grumbled, interrupting his self-psycho-analyzing.

"I get first dibs on the glass of orange juice," Anna declared.

"Did Parnell call the office today?" He passed her the juice. "Mary phoned and said he was meeting with his Gamblers Anonymous coach."

"A gambling coach, huh?" Ryan plopped a red grape into her mouth.

"Bobby got on the phone and told me to clean out his office. Keep the business contracts in my desk, but get rid of everything else."

She motioned for another grape. "It's weird, but I got the impression that Bobby wasn't coming back for a while."

"Maybe his coach thought he wasn't ready."

"Possibly." Anna smoothed her hand over Ryan's chest and stomach, then poked her finger inside his belly button.

"Stop, you little tease." He held her finger prisoner.

"Ryan?"

"What?"

"Will you tell me your real name?"

The oxygen in his lungs froze.

"And it wasn't the Lexus, the apartment in Manhattan or the hotel room in Atlantic City that gave you away. I suspected you were using an alias when I filled out your employment forms the first day on the job."

Anna hadn't survived the foster-care system without learning to read people. He wouldn't insult her by lying. "It's Ryan McKade."

"McKade. A strong-sounding Irish name."

Caught off guard by her easy acceptance of his having kept his identity a secret, he was speechless.

"Tell me about your family," she coaxed.

"My family owns McKade Import-Export and I'm in charge of the New York office. I handle most of our European customers. My elder brother, Nelson, runs the Chicago branch and my younger brother, Aaron, handles the West Coast."

"Wow. Must be a big company if it takes three offices in three cities." Anna was impressed but not shocked that Ryan was a business bigwig. "That explains who you are and what you do for a living, but not why you showed up on the rubbish company's payroll."

Ryan smoothed the hair from her cheek. "Grandfather believed he'd been remiss in teaching me and my brothers life lessons."

"The old man sounds intriguing."

"He's a meddler. Anyway, the lesson I needed to learn was bravery."

"What?" Anna bolted upright and gaped. "That's outrageous."

"I appreciate your indignation, but Grandfather accused me of being a coward."

"Ridiculous. Is he senile? He doesn't remember that you saved a woman's life during 9/11?"

Ryan suspected that when Anna committed her heart to a man, she'd defend him to the death. "My grandfather meant well. He believed that I'd stopped living after 9/11. That my injuries, the divorce and the loss of my unborn child stole my will to live."

"You mean you contemplated suicide?"

He'd never told his grandfather or his brothers, but he owed Anna the truth. And much more. "Once. I considered downing a bottle of prescription pain meds with whiskey."

Tears blurred Anna's eyes. "What stopped you?"

"I don't remember." But he was damn glad he had stopped after taking four of the pills, or he'd never have met Anna. Never have experienced the joy of being with her. The possibility of a brighter future.

"Thank goodness you didn't, Ryan." She snuggled

against his side and pressed her cheek to his heart. "I wonder why your grandfather picked Parnell Brothers for you to hire on with. Have you asked him?"

"No, but maybe I should." Now that Anna had brought up the subject, he acknowledged that his grandfather never did anything on a whim. He suspected the old man had a definite reason for arranging Ryan's job at the station. "Grandfather believes forcing me to mingle with people will whisk me back to the world of the living."

"And has it?"

"Yes." Anna was proof it had.

Blue eyes shining with emotion, she asked, "Now that you've learned your lesson, in what direction is your life heading next?"

"I hope in yours, Anastazia Nowakowski." He set her orange-juice glass on the table. "I love you." He expected happiness, joy, elation…anything but her empty that gazed back at him.

Dear God. He was the only one in love.

HEART ACHING, Anna stood at the front window of her apartment, watching the night swallow Ryan's shadow. Sobs clogged her throat and she was thankful her roommate had decided to spend the evening elsewhere. She didn't want anyone disturbing her pity party.

After Ryan's declaration of love, he'd waited for her to confess her feelings. The anticipation in his eyes had faded to hurt when she'd remained silent. That he cared deeply for her was more than she could have wished for, more than she deserved. Lord, how she'd wanted to tell him she loved him. Instead, she'd kept the words inside, until they'd almost choked her. She had no right to declare her love when she doubted a happily-ever-after was in the picture for them. She'd been aware her silence had wounded him. Better he suffer now than later, after he learned she'd led him astray.

Better for whom, Anna? You or Ryan?

A man of strong principles, Ryan could forgive a lot of faults but not this one, she feared. She was certain that once he discovered she'd given up her daughter for adoption, he'd want nothing to do with her, and she refused to place him in a position of having to make up reasons for backing out of their relationship.

Why did Ryan have to be the one man who made her happy? Had she committed an unforgivable sin in giving her daughter away? Was this God's punishment—sentencing her to a lifetime of loneliness? Yes, she had friends and coworkers and Blair, but they would never replace the love of Ryan. Why did fate have to be so cruel as to bring Ryan into her life? Why did she have to experience the love and joy of such a wonderful man, merely to lose him forever? So many questions…

Tell him the truth. The whole truth. He might understand.

No. This was one time the truth would cause more pain, more sorrow. How could Ryan forgive her when she'd yet to forgive herself? Besides, it was too late for the truth. She should have brought up Tina in Atlantic City after he'd spilled his guts about his wife's miscarriage.

She attempted to console herself with the idea that even if Ryan managed to forgive her, they were from different worlds—different socioeconomic upbringings. She convinced herself that Ryan had readily assimilated with her blue-collar coworkers because he'd done it for his grandfather. Not because of any feelings he'd had for her. Even if their polar-opposite upbringings weren't an issue, she'd never be comfortable living in a high-rise condo or an apartment in Manhattan. She needed neighbors. Friends. A close-knit community around her. She belonged in Queens. Queens was where she would stay.

By herself.

Without Ryan.

Alone.

Chapter Thirteen

"Thank God." Anna popped out of the chair the moment Ryan stepped into the front office. She braced one hand on the mound of paperwork in the In basket and the other on her flat tummy, waiting for a menstrual cramp to ease. Exercise helped lessen the cramping and she should have taken a walk for lunch, instead of using the time to solicit local businesses to consider Parnell Brothers' services. But the company needed cash and quickly. Neither she nor Ryan would collect a paycheck for the week. The other men would receive half their pay.

"You're not…" Gaze glued to her stomach, Ryan crossed the room and stopped before her.

Pregnant? A sliver of hurt wedged itself in Anna's heart. After all he'd shared with her about his wife's miscarriage, how did he dare think she'd be so cruel as to intentionally keep a pregnancy from him? "No!"

He jumped at her firm pronouncement. Then his eyes connected with hers, and for an infinitesimal second she read regret in the brown orbs. She had regrets, too. A tiny part of her had hoped she'd become pregnant from the one time they'd made love without using protection.

She would have welcomed the excuse to have to make their relationship work for the baby's sake.

"Your face is as white as Blair's cake frosting," he commented.

Ever since they'd made love Monday night at her apartment, they'd tiptoed around each other as if one wrong word would spark their unspoken truce into flames. Although she cherished his declaration of love, she ached with regret at having hurt his pride and wounded his feelings. "A man in Bobby's office. He's been waiting to speak with you for over an hour."

"What's his name?"

"He didn't say. But he mentioned a person named Little Nicky." Anna clutched Ryan's arm, not caring the action bordered on melodrama. "He looks mean."

Crap. Ryan had hoped he'd have more time to resolve the situation with the mafia. Obviously the mob boss was dead serious about possessing the business. "Don't worry." The promise rang empty in his ears. "After I see what the guy wants, we'll grab a bite to eat." Sick and tired of the tension between them, he intended to have a long talk with Anna. He knew she loved him. Why she refused to confess her feelings puzzled Ryan. Whatever the reason, he was determined to uncover the answer tonight. He'd come this far with her—his heart was in too deep to walk away without a fight.

Then Ryan did what he'd been dying to do all week but hadn't—he kissed her. A brush of lips. When her sigh caressed his face, he moved away, afraid that if he kissed her the way he yearned to, the way he'd dreamed of, he'd never stop. He squeezed Anna's hand reassuringly, then went in search of Little Nicky's henchman.

Anna hadn't been kidding—Ryan had seen pit bulls

prettier than this guy's mug. As if the bone and cartilage had been smashed or removed, the mobster's nose lay flat against his face—two airholes above his lips barely visible. Pockmarks decorated his temples, cheeks and neck. Feet propped on the desk, he slouched in Bobby's chair and flashed a yellow-toothed sneer.

Deciding pleasantries weren't necessary, Ryan groused, "What do you want?"

"Boss sent me to remind you about the upcoming foreclosure."

November 5. The date had been in the back of Ryan's mind every minute of every hour. "I haven't forgotten."

"He expects everyone out by noon."

"Why the hurry?"

Mr. Goon popped the knuckles on one hand. "Boss plans to open the business right away."

Suspecting the mob's business had nothing to do with rubbish removal and a whole lot to do with loan-sharking, Ryan stated, "We need more time."

The size-thirteen boots disappeared from the top of the desk and banged against the floor. Ape-man stood, planted his beefy fists on the desk and growled, "You ain't got more time."

"More time for what?"

Both Ryan and the gorilla rotated their heads toward the softly voiced question. Anna stood in the doorway. "I'll explain later," Ryan warned.

"Well, now." Pancake Face moved out from behind the desk. "If the little missy needs a job real bad, the boss can put her to good use."

No matter how he might wish to defend Anna's honor, Ryan was no match for Godzilla. He caught Anna's eye and nodded to the door. The stubborn woman ignored him. Hands on her hips, chin in the air, she snapped at the bully, "What's going on?"

"We're shutting you down."

"What's he talking about?" Anna asked Ryan.

"Parnell sold out to Little Nicky."

Her gaze moved between the two men. "Who's Little Nicky?"

"He's Queens' mob boss," Ryan explained.

"Mob boss?" She pressed a palm to her heart. "What does the mafia want with a small-time garbage company?"

"Little Nicky don't share his plans with nobody. If you want a job, I'll put in a good word for—"

"She's not interested," Ryan interrupted. "Tell your boss the message was received." He slid an arm around Anna's waist and guided her to the chair in front of the desk.

"Noon." The goon sauntered out the door.

"Tell me it isn't true, Ryan." Anna's big blue eyes implored him.

Damn it. What the hell good did being filthy rich and possessing a powerful family name do if he couldn't save a garbage business from the hands of a sleaze like Little Nicky? He plowed his fingers through his hair. "Parnell put up the business as collateral for a loan from the mafia."

A moan escaped her mouth, the sound reminiscent of a wounded animal. "Start from the beginning," she whispered.

"After we found Parnell in Atlantic City and you left the hotel room to buy him a change of clothes, he confessed he'd borrowed against the business from the mob."

Trembling fingers covered her mouth and Ryan paused. When she motioned for him to continue, he added, "It wasn't the first time. I visited Little Nicky and discovered that my grandfather had paid off a previous debt Parnell owed in exchange for hiring me."

"Maybe your grandfather could pay—"

"I offered to clear Parnell's debt. McKade Import-Export could have absorbed the loss, but Little Nicky wouldn't budge."

Sniffle. "What will the mob do with the business?"

"Nothing. They'll use it as a front for illegal activity."

Anna rose from the chair, eyes pleading. "Don't let them take the business." Her fingernails bit into his skin, leaving half-moon marks on his forearm.

He wished he could be Anna's knight in shining armor and rescue the company from the clutches of the evil underworld. How could he save a woman from a burning building during a terrorist attack but not be able to save a garbage company from the mob? What the hell kind of sense did that make?

"Leon's got too many family members depending on him. He can't afford to lose his job. This morning Antonio's wife, Lisa, phoned to tell me she's pregnant." Anna's lower lip wobbled. "She hasn't told Antonio yet."

Typical Anna—worry about others and not herself. Ryan yanked her into his arms and tucked her face against his neck. He hugged her, hoping his strength would calm the tremors racking her body. "They're good men, sweetheart. They'll find new jobs."

After several muffled sniffles, she wiggled free. Arms wrapped around her middle, she whimpered, "They're my family. I don't want to lose them." Tears leaked from her eyes.

What about me? I want to be your family. Now wasn't the time to declare his feelings. "Anna, I wish I knew what to do."

"Can't you fix this?"

Her question knocked the breath from his lungs.

"Fix what?" Leon barged into the room—Joe, Eryk, Patrick and Antonio on his heels. The men ran their gazes over Anna's tear-stained face, then shifted their scowls to Ryan.

"Who's the creep that just left?" Patrick nodded to the window. Little Nicky's ape was getting into a car across the street.

"The guy works for a local mobster." Never in Ryan's life had he felt so inept.

"What business do you have with a mob boss, Jones?" Eryk glared.

"Not me. Parnell. Little Nicky's been funding his gambling habit."

Leon grasped Anna's arm. "Is he telling the truth?"

How could the older man question Ryan's integrity after they'd worked together for the past few months? Ticked, Ryan held his tongue.

"Yes," Anna answered.

"How much is Parnell in for?" Eryk made eye contact with each man in the room. "We can go two weeks— maybe three—without a paycheck."

That the men were willing to work without pay and make sacrifices that would affect their families humbled Ryan. It wasn't simply Anna who considered her fellow employees family—the men possessed the same feelings about one another and their boss. Ryan admired their loyalty and commitment. "Parnell owes over three hundred thousand." The men's stunned expressions would have been comical had the situation not been so dire.

Leon dropped into the chair Anna had vacated and

buried his face in his hands. Antonio moved away from the group. Joe's complexion paled. Eryk and Patrick gazed unseeingly out the office window.

The desperation in the room was palpable.

"How long before the mob moves in?" Leon asked.

"Monday, November 5. We have to be out by noon," Ryan informed the group.

"Use next week to look for new jobs." Anna grimaced. "No sense showing up here when there's no money to make payroll."

"Why weren't we told about the problem with the mob?" Imitating a schoolyard bully, Antonio fisted his hands, ready to defend his territory.

Because I thought I could fix this. Thought I could save the business without anyone the wiser. Guilt gnawed a hole through Ryan's gut. He'd misjudged his ability, been overconfident, and he'd failed. Before he had the opportunity to answer Antonio's question, Joe stepped forward. "Any chance you can help?"

"You donated two thousand dollars toward Willie's funeral expenses. We never asked where you got that kind of money, but—" Antonio glanced around the group "—we've always suspected you weren't really who you said you were."

"Yeah, Jones. You're the furthest thing from blue collar I've ever seen," Eryk added.

"Could you loan us the money to pay off the mob?" Patrick made eye contact with his coworkers. "We'd pay you back with interest."

"I offered to pay off the debt, but Little Nicky refused my money," Ryan explained.

After a lengthy silence, Joe asked, "Mind telling us who the hell you are, Jones?"

"My real name is Ryan McKade, not Ryan Jones. My family owns McKade Import-Export."

"Import-export, huh?" Eryk snarled. "What if you're in cahoots with Little Nicky to take over the business?"

"Ryan wasn't aware that Bobby had a gambling problem until I told him," Anna said, jumping to his defense. "If anyone is to blame, it's me. I should have addressed the issue when I noticed the missing funds."

Refusing to allow her to believe Parnell's gambling habits had been her fault, Ryan grasped her hands. "Bobby has an addiction. Nothing you could have said would have deterred him." Life wasn't fair. Wasn't kind. "Hell, Anna. Shit happens and sometimes we can't do a damn thing about it."

"I could have confronted him," she argued.

The men encircled Anna. "This isn't your fault. You've taken good care of us over the years," Patrick argued. He motioned around the room. "Is the mob keeping everything?"

"'Fraid so," Ryan muttered. "Better clear your lockers or Little Nicky's enforcers will claim anything left behind."

RYAN PAUSED in the hallway outside the locker room and listened to the muted sounds of cussing. Anna had decided to rummage through Parnell's files and retrieve financial statements and other documents that would be needed at tax time. She'd declined his offer to help, and he schlepped off feeling as if he'd struck out and lost the game for his team.

"Can I speak with you guys a minute?" Ryan stepped into the locker room.

No one paid him any attention. Eryk was in the

process of removing a stack of yellowed newspapers from the top shelf of his locker. The other men were in various stages of organizing their personal belongings. A dirty sock sailed past Ryan's face, landing in the trash can by the door.

"I need a favor," he persisted.

Leon paused from examining a dent in his lunch box. "What kind of favor?"

"I want all of you to promise you'll keep in touch with Anna. You're her family now."

"What are you talking about?" Antonio spoke up. "None of us is related to Anna."

Was Antonio that obtuse, or did he really not *get it?* "Has Anna told you guys about her past?"

A hush fell over the room. The men glanced sideways at one another, then Joe scratched his head. "I don't remember Anna ever saying anything personal about herself. Do you guys?"

A chorus of grunts answered.

Ryan shouldn't divulge Anna's past, but if he couldn't save the business, maybe he could save her relationship with her coworkers. "Anna grew up in the foster-care system. When she was four years old, her mother died. She never met her father." He omitted the gory details. If the men cared to learn more, they could question Anna.

"How come Anna never said anything to us?" Leon posed the question to the group as if Anna's background was one of the great mysteries of the world.

"She was always fussing over us and our families." Patrick shook his head sadly. "Never thought to ask her about her folks."

"Yeah," Eryk mumbled. "And she was so cheerful and happy all the time I figured her life was fine."

The genuine misery etched on the men's faces assured Ryan they'd make an effort to involve Anna in their lives. "Please don't lose touch with her."

"Anna loves birthdays, so we'll invite her to our kids' parties," Antonio declared. The others chimed in with assurances that they'd include her in their family gatherings. Ryan was confident the men wouldn't neglect her.

"You're in love with her, aren't you?" Leon blurted after the room quieted.

The urge to deny the charge never materialized. "I am." Ryan had recognized his feelings for Anna had become serious when he'd experienced a jealous zap several weeks ago after witnessing her straighten Blair's tie on the apartment stoop. He never thought those feelings would develop into love. But Anna was an amazing woman.

"So you'll be her family, too." Antonio lifted a dark eyebrow, as if Ryan was a dope.

"I'll be resuming my job in Manhattan."

"If you love her, you can't let her go," Joe protested.

"It's not me who's letting go. Anna doesn't love me." He had no intention of discussing his failed love life with the guys. "If she should ever need anything—" Ryan dug out his wallet, removed a business card and handed it to Leon "—call me and I'll do what I can."

"She cares about you," Joe insisted. "Maybe you should stick around awhile longer and see if anything changes between you two."

Ryan had yet to respond to Joe's suggestion when Eryk held up one of the yellowed newspapers from his locker. "I thought you looked familiar when you first showed up here." He passed the front page of the *Times* to Leon.

The others crowded around and gawked over Leon's shoulder. "Is that you?" Eryk stabbed his finger at the picture of Ryan carrying a woman out of the second tower during the 9/11 attack.

The picture itself was photojournalism perfection. Ryan's suit coat was on fire, the flames shooting into the air in the shape of angel wings. Thinking back, he couldn't remember feeling any pain as he'd cradled the woman against his chest and stumbled from the building. "Yeah, that's me."

Collapsing onto the stool next to his locker, Eryk buried his face in his hands. He muttered a litany of swearwords, then glanced up, face wet with tears.

The man's emotional reaction caught Ryan off guard and he mumbled, "It was no big deal. She was just a woman who couldn't get out on her own."

"Just a woman?" Eryk's voice hitched.

The walls closed in around Ryan. The guys gaped at him as if he were an apparition. Eryk snatched the paper from Leon's grasp and rattled it. "That wasn't just a woman, Jones, McKade, whoever the hell you are." He sucked in a deep breath and bellowed, "You saved my sister-in-law!"

Oh God. The woman Ryan had rescued had been the sister-in-law whose kids Eryk and his wife babysat for one weekend a month so that the woman and her husband could spend time alone. Ryan's mind drifted to an exchange with his grandfather.

"Why a rubbish company, Grandpa? Anything but garbage."

"You have to face the past, Ryan."

Everything made sense now. His grandfather's insistence that Ryan work for Parnell Brothers. He must have met Valerie and her family at the hospital when Ryan had refused to see her. His grandfather's cunning astounded him.

"Why wouldn't you talk to Valerie?" Eryk raged. "Because of you, her children aren't motherless and her husband isn't a widower. She wanted to thank you for saving her life, but you refused to see her."

Shame filled Ryan. The pain from his injuries had been so intense that the first few weeks in the hospital he'd regretted going into the second tower when he'd heard Valerie's cries for help. Later, after he'd learned of Sandra's miscarriage, he'd hated himself, the whole world, even Valerie. And why shouldn't he have? Valerie's life had returned to normal and his had crumbled.

After becoming better acquainted with Eryk and learning how deeply he cared for his family, Ryan could no longer regret saving the man's sister-in-law. "I was in a lot of pain and I—"

"How bad were you injured?" Eryk cut him off. "The doctors refused to say."

"I'm here, aren't I?" Ryan joked.

No one laughed.

Time to leave. He moved toward the door, but Eryk blocked his way. "That's it? No explanation?"

"What do you want me to say?" Ryan shouted, startling the men.

Anger at his grandfather for meddling in his and other people's lives raged through Ryan. "I saved your sister-in-law, and because I did, I lost my wife and my unborn child. How's that for something to say?"

He stormed from the room, hating that his grandfather had been right—he was a damn coward.

Chapter Fourteen

"Hello?"

"Grandpa, it's me, Ryan. You play dirty, don't you?" The combination of anger and acid building in his stomach made Ryan want to puke.

"I assume this call isn't about coming up on the short end of the stick with Little Nicky."

"How did you find out I failed to save Parnell Brothers from the mob?"

"The Polish girl phoned me."

"Anna?"

Ryan had hit rock bottom yesterday when he'd left Parnell Brothers after his parting shot in the locker room. He'd hoped—no, expected—Anna to knock on his apartment door to check on him. She hadn't. Hadn't phoned, either. Leaving Ryan confused. Lonely. And scared. Scared of losing Anna. Of losing a second chance at living.

"Anna thought your family should be told that the woman you'd rescued during 9/11 turned out to be one of your coworker's relatives. She said you were quite upset."

Ryan remembered the cruel words he'd spoken—

blaming Eryk's sister-in-law for the failure of his marriage and the loss of his unborn child. "Did you tell her that you'd orchestrated the whole thing?"

"Son, I believed the way to help you move forward with your life was to force you to confront the past head-on."

"That's why you sent me to Parnell Brothers."

"Yes. You needed to discover that a fair amount of good had been salvaged from that fateful day. Not all was lost."

"It's hard, Grandpa." Ryan closed his eyes. He was tired. So damn tired of fighting. Struggling. Surviving.

"You've blamed your ex-wife. You've blamed the woman you rescued. You've even blamed the terrorists. Easier than blaming yourself, isn't it?"

As if he'd been punched in the throat, Ryan felt his vision go gray and his head spin. "What do you mean?" he wheezed.

"I understand what you're going through. Those first ten years I blamed myself for the deaths of your parents and grandmother."

"The plane crash wasn't your fault, Grandpa."

"No, but I arranged the vacation. I noticed your father's long hours were putting a strain on his marriage. And your grandmother worried about me working myself to death and dying of a heart attack before the age of sixty. I assumed a weekend ski trip would appease everyone. But before your father and I left the office, a problem developed with one of our clients. I insisted on staying behind and promised to catch a flight in the morning. By then they were all dead."

Ryan's throat tightened. As far as he remembered, his grandfather had never spoken in length about the tragic plane crash.

"You never forget. And the pain never goes away."

"But you were attempting to do the right thing," Ryan argued.

"I'm ninety-one years old and I still haven't figured out God's rules for the game of life. If you find the answer to why innocent, good people die before nasty evildoers, clue me in."

Ryan thought of his unborn child. He'd instigated the argument with Sandra. He'd been the one to offend her. To say terrible things. He'd meant to hurt her. He hadn't meant to hurt the baby. In the end he'd ended up hurting himself the most. "What if I can't let go?"

"You don't have to let go. You just have to move on. In the beginning you do it because others are depending on you. Later, after navigating years of pain, you understand and accept that life is a gift and not to be wasted."

Rubbing a hand beneath his runny nose, Ryan sniffed. "Some hero I am, crying like a baby."

"You are a hero, Ryan. But not the way you assume."

"What do you mean?"

"My boy, you're a hero because it takes more courage to live your life now than it did before 9/11. Before losing your marriage. Before losing your child. A hero is courageous and strong. And *human*. You feel pain, fear and hurt from your heroic actions." His grandfather cleared his throat.

"You possess a deep well of courage, my boy. Look inside yourself and use your stubbornness, persistence and firmness of will to lend you the guts not just to live but to thrive. To experience life to the fullest. To triumph over adversity."

"What should I do about Parnell Brothers? It's too late to save—"

"Forget the garbage company," his grandfather interrupted. "The real issue is whether you're brave enough to save yourself."

Stunned, Ryan gaped at the receiver. A few seconds passed, then his grandfather whispered, "No matter what, I love you." The dial tone buzzed in Ryan's ear. He pressed the off button, then placed the phone on the nightstand.

Brave enough to save yourself...

A picture of Anna's sweet face flashed through his mind. He wanted her. Wanted all that she represented— love, forgiveness...life. He refused to walk away from her until he figured out the reason she believed they couldn't be together. Ryan suspected Anna had a past of her own to deal with.

But first, he had unfinished business with Little Nicky.

"You again?" Little Nicky puffed on his cigar.

Wearing a suit that Ryan hoped would lend him an air of serious determination, he stepped inside the mafia boss's office. He'd never challenged the mob before and prayed the action he'd taken earlier in the week wouldn't land him six feet under.

"Don't attempt to talk me out of taking possession of that rubbish company," the bully warned, one corner of his mouth lifting in a smirk. "I'm no champion for the underdog. Parnell may be a good man, but he's stupid."

With a nonchalance Ryan didn't feel, he slipped a paper from his suit-coat pocket and held it out.

Little Nicky grunted, then heaved his barrel chest forward and snatched the form. Two thick eyebrows dipped across his broad forehead as he scanned the contents of the letter. "This is bullshit." He crumpled the note in his fist, then fired it at the trash can in the corner. The paper wad hit the edge and bounced off, landing on the floor. "The McKade name may carry weight in Manhattan, but—" the goon lowered his voice "—*my* name rules Queens."

"I'm aware of your power and influence, as I am of your reputation for fairness."

At Ryan's pronouncement, some of the sizzle drained from Little Nicky's expression. "Go on."

"The first time we met I noticed you possessed a fair amount of integrity."

"Integrity!" The mobster laughed.

"You could have charged Parnell an exorbitant interest rate on his gambling loans, but you didn't. And you could have refused to allow my grandfather to pay off Parnell's debt a couple of months ago and seized the rubbish company then. Instead, you offered Parnell a second chance. I believe you're a fair man. As fair as a mob boss can be."

Seconds ticked by in silence, then Little Nicky muttered, "Ballsy move, McKade."

Ryan grinned. "I know."

"So you expect me to honor that?" The mobster motioned to the crumpled paper.

"The property, minus the trucks and equipment, has been appraised at just over half a million. More than Parnell owes you."

"I have connections in high places that can make that appraisal go away," the man threatened.

"But you won't do that."

"Because of my integrity." Hairy-knuckled fingers stubbed out the cigar. "Fine. Parnell can keep his trucks and equipment. But everything had better be gone from the building by noon tomorrow. Anything left behind belongs to me."

"Understood."

"What do I need with a dump truck," Little Nicky grumbled.

"I doubt you could launder money in it."

The mobster frowned, but his eyes glinted with humor. "Get the hell out of my office, McKade. And you'd better not show that pretty-boy face of yours around here again."

Feeling more optimistic than he had in a long, long time, Ryan left Mo's Tavern. He hadn't saved the building, but Parnell, Anna and the others had the trucks and equipment if they wanted to begin a new venture—a venture he was more than willing to help them get off the ground.

"ANNA, OPEN UP!" Ryan pounded his fist above the peephole in her apartment door. A moment later, the door swung open and a harried Blair appeared, wearing a gray suit with a white dress shirt, and a bright purple tie slung around his neck.

"Thank God." Anna's roommate retreated and motioned Ryan inside. "Ryan to the rescue," he muttered, fumbling with the tie.

After shutting the door, Ryan said, "Let me." He stepped forward and in a matter of seconds had Blair's tie straightened and the knot perfectly centered. "Before my garbage-collection gig I wore a suit and tie to work."

"Thanks." Blair hurried into the dining room and studied his reflection in the antique mirror. "Perfect." He headed for the kitchen. "I'm running late."

"Late for what?" Ryan followed.

"The opening of Chez Lei in Long Island." Blair searched through a kitchen drawer, removed a utensil and grinned. "I'm their new pastry chef and this is my lucky spatula." He kissed the rubber tip.

Amused by the man's antics, Ryan offered, "Congratulations."

"Thanks." Blair motioned toward the hallway that led to the bedrooms. "She's packing."

"Packing?" Ryan's heart beat double time. Ryan made a beeline for her bedroom, Blair nipping at his heels.

When they reached Anna's closed door, Blair pushed past Ryan and entered the room without knocking. "You've got company," he announced, then left Ryan on his own.

Clothes strewn about, duffel bags tossed on the bed, shoes piled on the floor outside the closet and a barrage of toiletries and makeup stacked on the dresser—the room was a disaster. Ryan hovered in the doorway, observing the mess.

With her back to him, Anna stuffed several pairs of jeans into an overnight bag. "I was expecting you, Eryk. The other guys already dropped by to talk me out of leaving. I appreciate the concern, but I'm not a child who needs watching over. I'm a grown woman who knows what she wants." She whirled, then squawked when her gaze landed on Ryan.

"And I'm a grown man who knows what he wants." His gaze traveled over Anna's face and body. Her eyes were puffy, as if she'd been crying. Hair mussed as if she'd rolled out of bed that morning and had neglected to brush it. Clothes rumpled as if… Lord, he'd missed her.

Blood pounding through her veins, Anna forced herself to take a deep, calming breath. That Ryan had sought her out lent her hope. She'd never been the kind of woman to chase a man, but Ryan wasn't just any man.

He was her man. And she wouldn't give him up without a fight. "I've missed you," she whispered.

He sagged against the door frame. His obvious relief brought tears to her eyes. She hated herself for what she'd put him through this past week. Why had it taken her so long to find the courage to tell him the truth?

"I imagine the guys told you about the not-so-nice things I said to Eryk."

"Eryk's very distressed. But not because of what you said." Anna ached to hug him.

"He's not?" The doubt on his face made her heart ache.

"I explained to him what had happened between you and Sandra and her miscarriage. Eryk wants to talk to you, Ryan. So do Valerie and her husband. They're all worried about you. They're all grieving for your loss."

"My grandfather said you'd called him."

"Your family loves you." She swallowed hard. "I love you."

"Then…" He motioned to the luggage on the bed. "Why are you packing?"

"I'm going home." *I hope.*

"I thought the guys at the station were your family."

"They're my extended family." She inched closer. "I've finally figured out why I've always lived on the fringe of other people's lives."

"Why's that?" He lifted his hand to her cheek and caressed her skin.

"Because pretending to be part of the group was safer than asking to come inside and risk being rejected." She nuzzled his warm, callused palm. "I'm ready to ask to come inside, Ryan." *Go on, you can do this.* "First, I have a confession to make. What I have to say may affect the way you feel about me."

"Whatever it is, Anna, it can't be as bad as—"

She pressed her fingers to his lips. "Please. It will be all the harder if you change your mind about me…about us." She motioned to the bed. "Have a seat."

This can't be good. Forcing himself to stay relaxed, he moved aside a pile of lingerie and sat. She stood across the room—biting her lip, her blue eyes wide. Worried. He wanted to hug her, to assure her that anything she'd done in the past didn't matter. Their future was more important.

"When I was fourteen, I got pregnant."

Anna was a mother? That was the last thing he'd expected her to confess.

"Michael, my boyfriend at the time, was seventeen and also a foster-care kid. He didn't want anything to do with me or the baby when he found out."

How sad. Ryan pictured a young Anna pregnant, abandoned by the baby's father and no family to lean on. "What did you do?" He suspected the answer. What choice did a girl in her situation have but to seek an abortion?

"My caseworker encouraged me to have an abortion, but I refused. My foster parents wouldn't allow me to stay with them if I didn't have the abortion, so I ran away."

Now he could add homeless to the image of Anna he'd formed in his mind.

Tears blurred her eyes. "I was scared, but in my heart I couldn't get rid of my baby. The third night I'd slept on the streets, I began cramping. I went to the emergency room and a nurse took pity on me. She contacted a woman who ran a home for unwed pregnant girls. The lady picked me up. While I was pregnant, I received good medical care, food, shelter and was even home-schooled so I didn't fall behind in my classes."

Ryan was relieved at the news that Anna hadn't been completely abandoned by the system.

"But there was a condition. The only way I would be granted refuge in the home was if I agreed to give up my baby for adoption."

Adoption?

"In my heart—" her voice cracked "—I believe I did the right thing. I couldn't have offered Tina much of a life." Her chin jutted as if she anticipated an argument from him.

"I'm so sorry, honey." He went to her. Wrapped her tight in his arms.

"You probably think I'm a terrible person—"

"No." He kissed her forehead. "I only hear love for your child in your voice. You granted her a gift no one else could have—you gave her life, Anna. Your daughter has you to be grateful for that."

"After losing your own child, I didn't think you'd understand how I could give mine away."

"You're a brave woman, Anastazia Nowakowski." He held her face to his neck and nuzzled the top of her head, breathed in her womanly scent. "Have you kept track of your daughter through the years?"

"Sort of. My caseworker broke a lot of rules for me. She slipped a letter I'd written to my daughter after she was born into Tina's file, and a picture of me holding Tina at the hospital. She also keeps my contact information current so that if Tina ever wants to find me, she can."

"Has she tried?"

"Not yet. She turned eighteen the night we went to DiRisio's."

He snapped his fingers. "Tina was the secret you were going to tell me that night, but Isabella and her husband interrupted you."

"You remember that?"

"I remember every time I was with you, Anna." His brown eyes warmed. "Have you discovered anything about the family who adopted her?"

"Not much. The couple live in one of the city boroughs. I'm glad my daughter had the family I always wished for."

"Someday she'll thank you for that in person."

"Do you think she'll ever let me be a part of her life?" Anna asked.

"Our life, Anna." He smiled. "If Tina wishes to be a part of our family, she will always be welcome."

"Are you saying what I assume you're saying?"

"Yes." He hugged her fiercely, burying his face in her neck. "I love you, Anna. Please say you'll marry me."

"Yes, yes, yes! I love you so much. I wanted to tell you that afternoon in my bed, but I was frightened."

"Of what?" He brushed a strand of hair from her cheek.

"Afraid you wouldn't understand why I gave Tina away. You'd already lost a child of your own and you'd said—"

"I remember what I said," he cut her off. "That I didn't understand how a mother could abandon her child."

Anna nodded.

"You didn't abandon Tina. You guaranteed her a better future. A future you wouldn't have been able to provide for her at the time."

"Thank you for understanding, Ryan. I've dreamed about the future with you. Having our own family." She snuggled closer.

"Will the guys at the station approve?" he asked.

"I'll promise to stay in touch with them after I move to Manhattan—"

"Screw Manhattan. We'll live in Queens. Right here in your apartment."

"Really?" Her face brightened.

"I want us to remain involved with the guys and their families. I've kept myself apart from my grandfather and brothers for too many years. I'm ready to be around people again. Besides, you can't live in Manhattan."

"I can't?"

Ryan shook his head. "I convinced Little Nicky to relinquish the company trucks and equipment. If you, Parnell and the others agree, you can establish a new rubbish-removal company somewhere else in Queens."

Anna squealed and flung her arms around his neck.

"But you're handling the books," Ryan declared.

"What about your job?"

"I can work from anywhere."

"The guys and I will keep an eye on Bobby." Her brow furrowed. "We'll have to buy a new garage for the trucks and equipment."

"McKade Import-Export will finance the business until you and the others get it off the ground. I'll guarantee you meet payroll until you're established," Ryan assured her.

"Oh, this is wonderful." Anna clapped her hands in excitement.

"I second that." Blair stood in the hallway, eavesdropping. "Anna, I've been waiting for the right time to mention this…."

"What?" She peered around Ryan's shoulder.

"Thatcher asked me to move in with him and I'm sure he's the one." Blair grinned.

Wiggling free of Ryan's embrace, Anna hugged Blair. "I'm happy for you. I've always approved of Thatcher."

Blair winked at Ryan. "You can use my bedroom as a nursery."

"Promise me that you and Thatcher won't be strangers," Anna insisted.

"You'll need babysitters, won't you?" Blair waved, then walked off.

When the front door slammed, Ryan sputtered, "Babysitters?"

On tiptoe, Anna kissed Ryan's cheek. "How do you feel about trying to have a child?"

Fatherhood. If his brothers could do it, then so could he. "Yeah, I'd enjoy raising a kid or two."

"I was counting on you saying that. We have so much love stored inside us, Ryan. We'll be wonderful parents."

"I hate to think where I'd be right now if my grandfather hadn't meddled in my life. You showed me that life is worth living. I'll do my best to be the kind of man you deserve. The kind of man you need. The kind you dream of."

"You don't have to try, Ryan. You already are that man." She clasped his face between her hands and brought his mouth to hers.

In her kiss Ryan discovered the forgiveness, compassion and acceptance he'd been searching for. With Anna by his side, he'd find the courage to weather life's ups and downs. The courage to accept himself for who he was—flaws and all. "When I'm with you, I feel like the bravest man in the world."

Her smile went straight to his heart. "You are the bravest...my hero. My love. My life."

Epilogue

"Zycze wam wszystkiego najlepszego na nowej drodze zycia."

Patrick McKade raised his glass to the group of wedding guests mingling in the reception hall.

Ryan tucked his new bride, Anna, against his side and listened to the old man translate the traditional Polish wedding toast.

"I wish you all of the best on your new road through life." A chorus of cheers followed, accompanied by clanking champagne and vodka glasses.

"I feel so blessed to be a part of your family." Anna gifted him with one of her smiles. He remembered how her smiles had driven him nuts when he'd first arrived at Parnell Brothers. Now he couldn't imagine a day without seeing a hundred of them.

Pride swelled in Ryan's chest as he searched for his brothers among the eclectic group of wedding guests. Nelson stood sentry over the beer keg at the back of the room after having caught his teenage stepson, Seth, trying to sneak a sip of alcohol. Nelson and his wife, Ellen, had made a minivacation out of their trip to New York. According to Ryan, Seth had spent his entire childhood milking cows and had never been out of the state of Illinois.

Nelson's wife chatted with Leon's family. The stocky German clan dwarfed his petite sister-in-law. Although Ellen insisted she was finished with dairy farming and was now busy working on her real estate license, Nelson confided to his brothers that he was keeping an eye out for a piece of good dairy farmland. Ryan suspected his elder brother had become fond of black-and-white bovines.

"Time for the money dance," Eryk shouted, then proceeded to demonstrate the dance custom by lifting the edge of his sister-in-law, Valerie's, bridesmaid dress. Then his brother put a headlock on Eryk and threatened to choke him. After having gotten better acquainted with the Gorski clan, Ryan could testify that he'd never met a family who argued more or loved as passionately.

"They're waiting for us." Anna tugged Ryan to the middle of the dance floor. The band struck up a polka and couples twirled around them.

Ignoring the music and the dancers, Ryan gazed into Anna's big blue eyes. "Thank you for loving me. For making my life worth living again. Because of you—" he held her hand to his heart "—the sun shines brighter in here. I love you, Mrs. McKade." He kissed her and the guests whooped and hollered.

"I'd be lost without you, too, Ryan."

They held hands and grinned at the slightly inebriated guests enjoying the Polish custom of circling the bride and groom.

"Have you ever seen such a beautiful baby?" Anna nodded to Aaron's wife, Jennifer, who stood near the buffet table, holding six-month-old Kathleen, named for Aaron, Nelson and Ryan's mother.

The kid brother no one thought would grow up and learn the meaning of responsibility was the first of the McKade men to become a father. "We're having all boys," Ryan whispered in Anna's ear.

"I'll give you as many boys as you want, as long as I have one little girl." Anna rose on tiptoe and kissed his cheek. He hoped they'd be blessed with several children because he wanted Anna to have the family she'd always dreamed of. And he hoped that with time, Tina would find her way back to them.

"Take off her veil, Ryan," Bobby Parnell shouted. The rubbish-company owner had made great progress in dealing with his gambling addiction. He and his wife were still separated, but Mary had agreed to hold off filing for divorce for one year. Parnell now worked side by side with Eryk, Antonio, Joe, Patrick and Leon at their new location in north Queens. Anna ran the office and managed the books.

"I guess we'd better do as they ask before one of the guests rips the veil off your head," Ryan complained. Who'd have thought Polish wedding guests could be so obnoxious. Carefully, Ryan removed the decorative pins holding Anna's headpiece in place. He spread the gauzy material across his arms and waltzed around the circle, catching the dollar bills and coins thrown by the well-wishers. Of all the Polish customs he'd been introduced to, this one was his favorite. Tradition said the money was to be used to help pay for the couple's honeymoon. Anna hadn't been told yet, but Ryan was surprising her with a trip to Europe.

The circle opened to allow Nelson and Aaron inside. Side by side, they dug out their wallets. Nelson removed a hundred-dollar bill and tossed it onto the veil. Not to be outdone, Aaron copied his eldest brother, and added an extra hundred.

"Oh, no, you don't," Nelson grumbled, throwing more money.

"Says who?" Aaron matched his brother's contribution.

And so it went until both brothers had emptied their wallets and stood gaping, dumbfounded, at each other.

Ryan handed the veil to Eryk's sister-in-law for safe-keeping, then slung his arms around his brothers' shoulders. "I thought Grandfather had lost his mind when he decided to teach each of us a life lesson. Not anymore." Ryan shifted his attention to Anna, who now stood sandwiched between his sisters-in-law, Ellen and Jennifer.

"Another toast!" Ryan's grandfather insisted, holding his companion, Mrs. Padrõn, close. A hush fell over the room as Patrick McKade lifted his champagne glass, then gazed adoringly at the woman by his side. "Here's to life lessons and the women who teach them!"

* * * * *

Look for an all-new miniseries
from Marin Thomas
HEARTS OF APPALACHIA
Launching October 2007 with
FOR THE CHILDREN
Only from Harlequin American Romance!

Welcome to cowboy country....

Turn the page for a sneak preview of
TEXAS BABY
by Kathleen O'Brien
An exciting new title from Harlequin Superromance
for everyone who loves stories about the West.

Harlequin Superromance—
Where life and love weave together in
emotional and unforgettable ways.

CHAPTER ONE

CHASE TRANSFERRED his gaze to the road and identified a foreign spot on the horizon. A car. Almost half a mile away, where the straight, tree-lined drive met the public road. He could tell it was coming too fast, but judging the speed of a vehicle moving straight toward you was tricky.

It wasn't until it was about two hundred yards away that he realized the driver must be drunk...or crazy. Or both.

The guy was going maybe sixty. On a private drive, out here in ranch country, where kids or horses or tractors or stupid chickens might come darting out any minute, that was criminal. Chase straightened from his comfortable slouch and waved his hands.

"Slow down, you fool," he called out. He took the porch steps quickly and began walking fast down the driveway.

The car veered oddly, from one lane to another, then up onto the slight rise of the thick green spring grass. It just barely missed the fence.

"Slow down, damn it!"

He couldn't see the driver, and he didn't recognize this automobile. It was small and old, and couldn't have cost much even when it was new. It was probably white, but now it needed either a wash or a new paint job or both.

"Damn it, what's wrong with you?"

At the last minute, he had to jump away, because the idiot behind the wheel clearly wasn't going to turn to avoid a collision. He couldn't believe it. The car kept coming, finally slowing a little, but it was too late.

Still going about thirty miles an hour, it slammed into the large, white-brick pillar that marked the front boundaries of the house. The pillar wasn't going to give an inch, so the car had to. The front end folded up like a paper fan.

It seemed to take forever for the car to settle, as if the trauma happened in slow motion, reverberating from the front to the back of the car in ripples of destruction. The front windshield suddenly seemed to ice over with lethal bits of glassy frost. Then the side windows exploded.

The front driver's door wrenched open, as if the car wanted to expel its contents. Metal buckled hideously. Small pieces, like hubcaps and mirrors, skipped and ricocheted insanely across the oyster-shell driveway.

Finally, everything was still. Into the silence, a plume of steam shot up like a geyser, smelling of rust and heat. Its snakelike hiss almost smothered the low, agonized moan of the driver.

Chase's anger had disappeared. He didn't feel anything but a dull sense of disbelief. Things like this didn't happen in real life. Not in his life. Maybe the sun had actually put him to sleep….

But he was already kneeling beside the car. The driver was a woman. The frosty glass-ice of the windshield was dotted with small flecks of blood. She must have hit it with her head, because just below her hairline a red liquid was seeping out. He touched it. He tried to wipe it away before it reached her eyebrow, though of course, that made no sense at all. Her eyes were shut.

Was she conscious? Did he dare move her? Her dress

was covered in glass, and the metal of the car was sticking out lethally in all the wrong places.

Then he remembered, with an intense relief, that every good medical man in the county was here, just behind the house, drinking his champagne. He found his phone and paged Trent.

The woman moaned again.

Alive, then. Thank God for that.

He saw Trent coming toward him, starting out at a lope, but quickly switching to a full run.

"Get Dr. Marchant," Chase called. "Don't bother with 911."

Trent didn't take long to assess the situation. A fraction of a second, and he began pulling out his cell phone and running toward the house.

The yelling seemed to have roused the woman. She opened her eyes. They were blue and clouded with pain and confusion.

"Chase," she said.

His breath stalled. His head pulled back. "What?"

Her only answer was another moan, and he wondered if he had imagined the word. He reached around her and put his arm behind her shoulders. She was tiny. Probably petite by nature, but surely way too thin. He could feel her shoulder blades pushing against her skin, as fragile as the wishbone in a turkey.

She seemed to have passed out, so he put his other arm under her knees and lifted her out. He tried to avoid the jagged metal, but her skirt caught on a piece and the tearing sound seemed to wake her again.

"No," she said. "Please."

"I'm just trying to help," he said. "It's going to be all right."

She seemed profoundly distressed. She wriggled in his arms, and she was so weak, like a broken bird. It made him feel too big and brutish. And intrusive. As if touching her this way, his bare hands against the warm skin behind her knees, were somehow a transgression.

He wished he could be more delicate. But he smelled gasoline, and he knew it wasn't safe to leave her here.

Finally he heard the sound of voices, as guests began to run around the side of the house, alerted by Trent. Dr. Marchant was at the front, racing toward them as if he were forty instead of seventy. Susannah was right behind him, her green dress floating around her trim legs.

"Please," the woman in his arms murmured again. She looked at him, the expression in her blue eyes lost and bewildered. He wondered if she might be on drugs. Hitting her head on the windshield might account for this unfocused, glazed look, but it couldn't explain the crazy driving.

"Please, put me down. Susannah… The wedding…"

Chase's arms tightened instinctively, and he froze in his tracks. She whimpered, and he realized he might be hurting her. "Say that again?"

"The wedding. I have to stop it."

* * * * *

Be sure to look for TEXAS BABY,
available September 11, 2007,
as well as other fantastic Superromance titles
available in September.

HARLEQUIN Super Romance®

Welcome to Cowboy Country...

TEXAS BABY

by *Kathleen O'Brien*

#1441

Chase Clayton doesn't know what to think.
A beautiful stranger has just crashed his
engagement party, demanding that he not
marry because she's pregnant with his baby.
But the kicker is—he's never seen her before.

Look for TEXAS BABY and other fantastic
Superromance titles on sale September 2007.

Available wherever books are sold.

HARLEQUIN Super Romance®

**Where life and love weave together
in emotional and unforgettable ways.**

REQUEST YOUR FREE BOOKS!
2 FREE NOVELS PLUS 2
FREE GIFTS!

American ROMANCE®

Heart, Home & Happiness!

YES! Please send me 2 FREE Harlequin American Romance® novels and my 2 FREE gifts. After receiving them, if I don't wish to receive any more books, I can return the shipping statement marked "cancel." If I don't cancel, I will receive 4 brand-new novels every month and be billed just $4.24 per book in the U.S., or $4.99 per book in Canada, plus 25¢ shipping and handling per book and applicable taxes, if any*. That's a savings of close to 15% off the cover price! I understand that accepting the 2 free books and gifts places me under no obligation to buy anything. I can always return a shipment and cancel at any time. Even if I never buy another book from Harlequin, the two free books and gifts are mine to keep forever.

154 HDN EEZK 354 HDN EEZV

Name	(PLEASE PRINT)	
Address		Apt. #
City	State/Prov.	Zip/Postal Code

Signature (if under 18, a parent or guardian must sign)

Mail to the **Harlequin Reader Service**®:
IN U.S.A.: P.O. Box 1867, Buffalo, NY 14240-1867
IN CANADA: P.O. Box 609, Fort Erie, Ontario L2A 5X3

Not valid to current Harlequin American Romance subscribers.

Want to try two free books from another line?
Call 1-800-873-8635 or visit www.morefreebooks.com.

* Terms and prices subject to change without notice. NY residents add applicable sales tax. Canadian residents will be charged applicable provincial taxes and GST. This offer is limited to one order per household. All orders subject to approval. Credit or debit balances in a customer's account(s) may be offset by any other outstanding balance owed by or to the customer. Please allow 4 to 6 weeks for delivery.

Your Privacy: Harlequin is committed to protecting your privacy. Our Privacy Policy is available online at www.eHarlequin.com or upon request from the Reader Service. From time to time we make our lists of customers available to reputable firms who may have a product or service of interest to you. If you would prefer we not share your name and address, please check here. ☐

HAR07

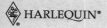

EVERLASTING LOVE™

Every great love has a story to tell™

Third time's a charm.

Texas summers. Charlie Morrison.
Jasmine Boudreaux has always connected
the two. Her relationship with Charlie
begins and ends in high school. Twenty
years later it begins again—and ends again.
Now fate has stepped in one more time—
will Jazzy and Charlie finally give in to
the love they've shared all this time?

Look for

Summer After Summer
by
Ann DeFee

Available September
wherever books are sold.

www.eHarlequin.com

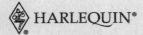

COMING NEXT MONTH

www.eHarlequin.com